AMERICA'S STORY

Historical Sources on Reconstruction

CHET'LA SEBREE AND ADRIANE RUGGIERO

Cavendish Square
New York

Published in 2020 by Cavendish Square Publishing, LLC
243 5th Avenue, Suite 136, New York, NY 10016

First Edition

Library of Congress Cataloging-in-Publication Data

Names: Sebree, Chet'la, author. | Ruggiero, Adriane, author.
Title: Historical Sources on Reconstruction / Chet'la Sebree and Adriane Ruggiero.
Description: First edition. | New York : Cavendish Square, 2020. |
Series: America's story | Includes bibliographical references and index.
Identifiers: LCCN 2018026115 (print) | LCCN 2018026511 (ebook) |
ISBN 9781502640857 (ebook) | ISBN 9781502640840 (library bound) |
ISBN 9781502640833 (pbk.)
Subjects: LCSH: Reconstruction (U.S. history, 1865-1877)--Juvenile literature.
Classification: LCC E668 (ebook) | LCC E668 .S45 2019 (print) | DDC 973.8--dc23
LC record available at https://lccn.loc.gov/2018026115

Editorial Director: David McNamara
Copy Editor: Nathan Heidelberger
Associate Art Director: Alan Sliwinski
Designer: Christina Shults
Production Coordinator: Karol Szymczuk
Photo Research: J8 Media

The photographs in this book are used by permission and through the courtesy of:
Cover George Barnard/Library of Congress/Wikimedia Commons/File:Atlanta roundhouse ruin3.jpg/Public Domain, (background and used throughout) Foxstudio/Shutterstock.com; p. 4, 43, 54, 91 Everett Historical/Shutterstock.com; p. 7 Archive Photos/Getty Images; p. 9 Library of Congress/Wikimedia Commons/File:Freedman's bureau.jpg/Public Domain; p. 10 Look and Learn/Bridgeman Images; p. 15 Currier and Ives/Library of Congress/Wikimedia Commons/File:Republican presidential ticket 1864b.jpg/Public Domain; p. 18 PhotoQuest/Archive Photos/Getty Images; p. 20 Matthew Brady/Library of Congress/Wikimedia Commons/File:President Rutherford Hayes 1870 1880 Restored.jpg/Public Domain; p. 22, 24, 73 Bettmann/Getty Images; p. 30 Harper's Weekly/Wikimedia Commons/File:AdoptionOf13thAmendment.jpg/Public Domain; p. 32 Alexander Gardner/Library of Congress/Wikimedia Commons/File:Abraham Lincoln giving his second Inaugural Address (4 March 1865).jpg/Public Domain; p. 38 Fotosearch/Archive Photos/Getty Images; p. 40, 50, 94 Corbis/Getty Images; p. 48, 109 Library of Congress; p. 65 Universal History Archive/UIG/Getty Images; p. 70 JPL Designs/Shutterstock.com; p. 87 Bildagentur-online/UIG/Getty Images; p. 101 Harris & Ewing/Library of Congress/Wikimedia Commons/File:Booker T Washington 16114a.jpg/Public Domain; p. 105 National Archives; p. 112 Keystone-France/Gamma-Keystone/Getty Images; p. 117 Stock Montage/Getty Images; p. 125 Library of Congress/Wikimedia Commons/File:Sharecropper Sam Williams with family members and laborers in cotton field LCCN98506914.tif/Public Domain; p. 129 By RonTech3000/Shutterstock.com.

Printed in the United States of America

AMERICA'S STORY

CONTENTS

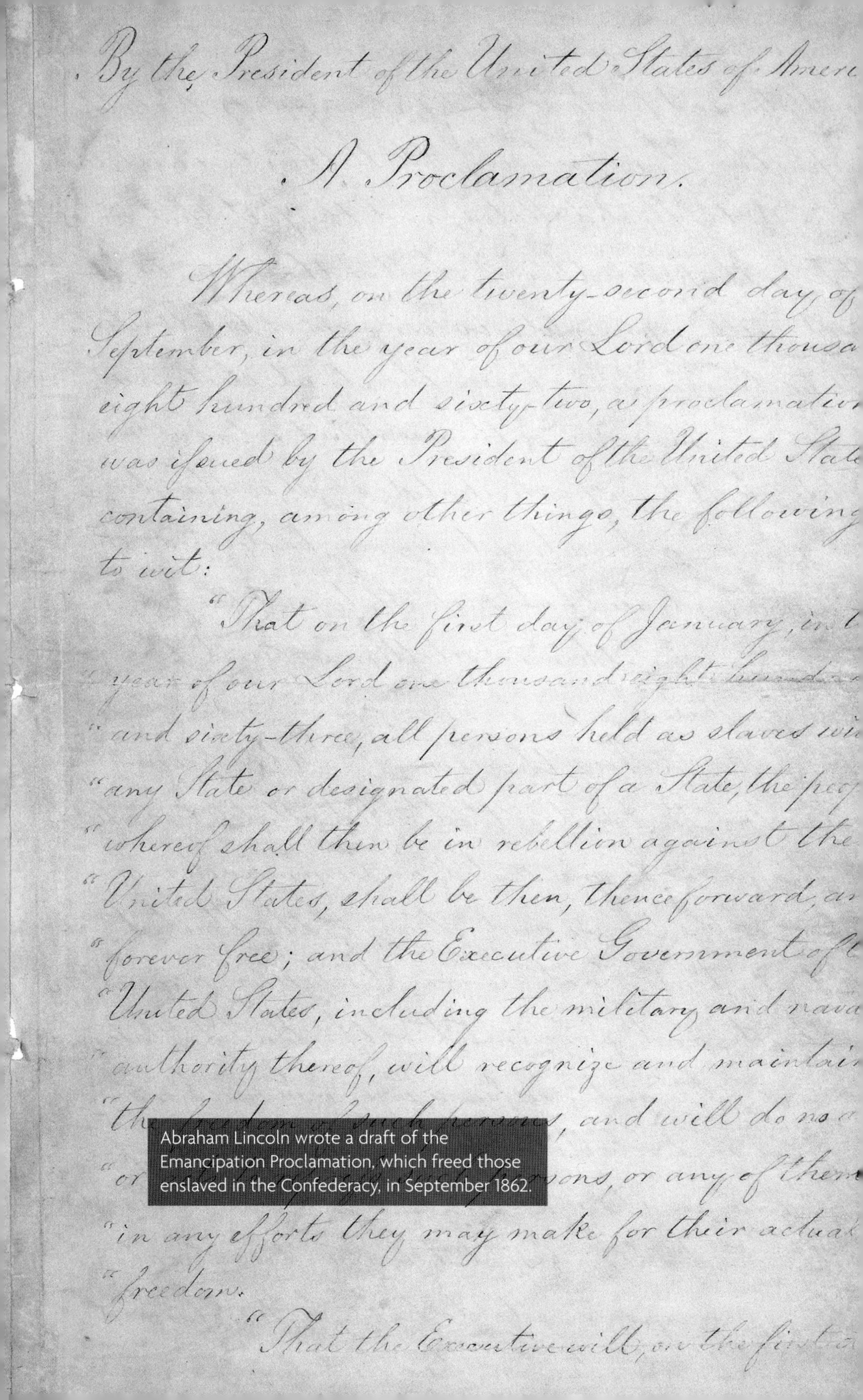

By the President of the United States of Amer[ica]

A Proclamation.

Whereas, on the twenty-second day of
September, in the year of our Lord one thousa[nd]
eight hundred and sixty-two, a proclamatio[n]
was issued by the President of the United State[s]
containing, among other things, the following
to wit:

"That on the first day of January, in t[he]
"year of our Lord one thousand eight hund[red]
"and sixty-three, all persons held as slaves wi[thin]
"any State or designated part of a State, the peo[ple]
"whereof shall then be in rebellion against the
"United States, shall be then, thenceforward, an[d]
"forever free; and the Executive Government of t[he]
"United States, including the military and nava[l]
"authority thereof, will recognize and maintai[n]
"the freedom of such persons, and will do no a[ct]
"or acts to repress such persons, or any of them
"in any efforts they may make for their actual
"freedom.

"That the Executive will, on the first [day]

Abraham Lincoln wrote a draft of the Emancipation Proclamation, which freed those enslaved in the Confederacy, in September 1862.

Primary Sources

In the pages that follow, you will hear from many different people from a time in America's past. These selections will vary in length. Some are long, and others are short. You'll find many easy to understand at first reading, but some may require several readings. All the selections have one thing in common, however. They are primary sources. They are important to us because they are the core material for all historical investigation.

What Is a Primary Source?

The term "primary source" is the name historians give to the information that makes up the record of human existence. A primary source is "history" itself. Primary sources are evidence. They give historians the all-important clues they need to understand the past.

Perhaps you have read a detective story in which an investigator has to solve a mystery by piecing together bits of evidence that he or she uncovers. The detective makes deductions, or educated guesses based on the evidence, and solves the mystery once all the deductions point in a certain direction. Historians work in much the same way. Like detectives, they analyze data through careful reading and rereading. After much analysis, they draw conclusions about an event, a person, or an entire era. Different historians may analyze the same evidence and come to different conclusions. That is why there is often strong disagreement about an event.

Primary sources are also called documents. It is a rather dry word to describe what can be just about anything: an official speech by a government leader, an old map, an act of Congress, a letter, a diary entry, a newspaper article, a song, a poster, a cartoon, a photograph, or someone captured on tape or film.

By examining the following documents, you will be taking on the role of historian. Here is your chance to jump into an important period in American history: the Reconstruction Era. This period lasted from the end of the Civil War in 1865 until the withdrawal of the last federal troops from the South in 1877. Some historians even argue that the era actually started as soon as Union soldiers arrived in slaveholding territory in 1861. Some argue that it lasted until the end of the nineteenth century. Collectively, however, everyone acknowledges that Reconstruction was a time when the nation was trying to rebuild itself after several states left the Union in the early 1860s.

Through primary sources, you will come to know the men and women who lived during that chaotic period. You will hear their points of view in the great debate that took place over how the nation should rebuild and reunite after the devastating war. You will read their often sharply opposing opinions on the meaning of freedom and the role the newly freed enslaved Africans should play in society.

This *Harper's Weekly* cartoon criticizes President Andrew Johnson's Reconstruction plans. For instance, it depicts Johnson as Iago from William Shakespeare's *Othello*—a play in which Iago betrays Othello, a black man.

How to Read a Primary Source

Each document in this book comes from Reconstruction or the years immediately preceding or following that period. Some documents are presidential papers. Others are selections from laws passed by Congress or state legislatures. There are speeches and accounts by politicians, military officers, laborers, newspaper editors, and former slave owners. These documents reflect the opinions of Americans on all sides of the Reconstruction debate. The book includes sources from people who pushed for radical reforms, or changes, and conservatives who denounced, or publicly declared as wrong, the federal government's actions as "tyranny," or an oppressive government. All of the documents help us to understand what it was like to live during the Reconstruction Era.

As you read each document, ask yourself some basic questions. Who is writing or speaking? Who is that person's intended audience? What is he or she trying to tell the audience? Is the message clearly expressed or is it implied—that is, stated indirectly? What words does the writer use to convey his or her message? Are the words emotional or objective in tone? These are questions that can help you think critically about a primary source.

There are also some tools in each chapter to help you unpack these documents. Some terms and concepts you may not be familiar with have been explained in sidebars. Also, questions follow each of the documents to help you focus and think through the primary source you have just read. As you read each selection, you'll probably come up with many questions of your own. That's great! The work of a historian always leads to many, many questions. Some can be answered, while others will require more investigation. Perhaps when you finish reading this book, your questions will lead you to further explorations of the Reconstruction Era.

Newspapers and political cartoons, like this one criticizing a government agency supporting Reconstruction in the South, are examples of primary sources.

This painting depicts General Robert E. Lee of the Confederacy surrendering to General Ulysses S. Grant of the Union at the Appomattox Court House in April 1865, effectively ending the Civil War.

INTRODUCTION

Reconstruction Plans and Responses

At the end of the Civil War, the South was a conquered, ruined land. The plantations that were the foundation of the Southern agricultural economy were destroyed. Cities, towns, and villages were covered with the wreckage of war. Millions of previously enslaved people and slave owners were scattered. Many of both groups were homeless and starving. Confederate governments had dissolved. Bandits roamed the land, looting, or stealing, at will. The only remaining authority was the Union army. Its victorious troops attempted to govern the South and hand out justice in military courts. Meanwhile, federal agents of the newly created Freedmen's Bureau struggled to provide aid and protect the freed slaves.

The Road to Civil War

The nation was fairly young when war erupted in the mid-nineteenth century. In the years that followed the American Revolution, which gave the United States its independence from the United Kingdom, the North and the South started to develop distinctly different economies. The Industrial Revolution led to the modernization of Northern states. They began to rely heavily on skilled laborers in factories. Conversely, the South had an agriculture-based economy. Southern plantation owners made money selling commercial crops like cotton and tobacco. For instance, the demand for cotton soared in the early to mid-nineteenth century, leading to rising cotton prices. These Southern plantations, however, were dependent on slave labor.

Opinions about slavery in the North and the South were almost as different as the region's economies. While there were still enslaved people in Northern states, many Northerners started to oppose slavery. Some of these people became abolitionists, or people who fought for the end of slavery. In the mid-nineteenth century, many of these people were also members of the newly founded Republican Party. They wanted to end—or at the very least, stop the expansion of—slavery. Meanwhile, Democrats, often Southerners, supported slavery and its expansion.

The tension between the desire to end and the desire to expand slavery became more of an issue as the young nation continued to grow. More territories were acquired by the United States either through war or purchase. For Southerners, this would mean more land on which they could grow crops. Laws like the Northwest Ordinance of 1787 and the Missouri Compromise made this difficult, though. These laws limited the expansion of slavery by making the institution illegal in certain territories. For instance, the Missouri Compromise made slavery illegal north of latitude

36°30′, except for in Missouri. Southerners were frustrated with the ways in which these laws affected their economy and way of live.

These tensions would continue to rise in the 1850s as abolitionists pushed for the end of slavery. In the midst of all of this, Kansas and Nebraska sought statehood. In accordance with the Missouri Compromise, both states should have been admitted to the Union as Free States since they were north of the specified latitude. However, according to the new Kansas-Nebraska Act of 1854, the question of whether or not the states would allow slavery would be determined by popular sovereignty, the process by which a state's citizens vote to make a decision. This led to a period known as Bleeding Kansas, where slavery advocates and abolitionists fought over the question of slavery in Kansas.

The 1860 presidential election, however, would change everything. Republican candidate Abraham Lincoln won over Democratic candidates John C. Breckinridge and Stephen A. Douglas, who sponsored the act that allowed Kansas and Nebraska's slavery status to be decided by popular sovereignty. Democrats saw Lincoln's election as a threat, as Republicans largely supported the abolition of slavery. They were determined to do something to preserve their way of life.

Before Lincoln was inaugurated, South Carolina seceded, or formally withdrew, from the Union. Six more states would follow suit before he moved into the White House. These states would go on to become the Confederate States of America, along with an additional four states. A month after Lincoln's inauguration in March 1861, the Civil War broke out between the Union and the seceded states. On April 12, 1861, Confederate soldiers fired the first shots on Union soldiers at Fort Sumter in South Carolina. The war would continue for four years. In the end, the Southerners were unsuccessful. The Confederacy would fall and slavery would be abolished.

Post–Civil War Tensions

With their old way of life destroyed and their land occupied by federal troops, white Southerners felt angry, afraid, and humiliated. To be fair, many Northerners were hostile, or aggressive, to people in the defeated Confederate states. They viewed Southerners as traitors. Northerners were determined to punish Southerners for seceding from the Union. They blamed Southerners for bringing on the devastating war. Other more reasonable voices in the North, however, spoke out for even-tempered justice.

The task facing the president was huge. He had to reunite the country. He was responsible for making sure that the South formed new state governments that were loyal to the Union. Additionally, he had to define the role of the formerly enslaved Africans in this newly reunited country.

President Abraham Lincoln's Plan and Congressional Responses

Long before the Civil War ended, however, Abraham Lincoln had begun to draw up a plan for Reconstruction. Although Lincoln opposed slavery, his main goal was to heal the wounds of war and restore the nation as quickly as possible. One of his primary focuses was to readmit the seceded states to the Union. His Reconstruction plan called for recognizing new Southern state governments after one-tenth of the state's voters agreed to renounce, or reject, slavery and to take an oath of loyalty to the Union.

Lincoln's moderate, or modest, plan worried a group of Republicans in Congress. They favored a more radical, or a more dramatic and fundamental, restructuring of Southern society. These Radical Republicans were led by two outspoken abolitionists, Thaddeus Stevens in the House of Representatives and Charles Sumner in the Senate. The Radicals called for far-reaching changes that would ensure that slave owners never returned to power.

INTRODUCTION: RECONSTRUCTION PLANS AND RESPONSES

This 1864 campaign banner depicts Republican presidential candidate Abraham Lincoln and his running mate, Democrat Andrew Johnson, who would become president after Lincoln's assassination in April 1865.

They wanted to replace the old plantation system of slaves and masters with a new society based on paid labor and equal rights. They also believed that Congress, and not the president, had the authority to apply a plan for Reconstruction.

Unfortunately, President Lincoln was assassinated, or killed for political reasons, in April 1865. He did not have the opportunity to put his Reconstruction plan into action. His vice president, Southern Democrat Andrew Johnson, inherited the difficult task of rebuilding the nation.

President Andrew Johnson's Plan

Robert E. Lee, a general of the Confederate Army, surrendered at the Battle of Appomattox on April 9, 1865. Days later, President Lincoln was assassinated, and Johnson became president. Although fighting continued in some areas for a couple more months, the Civil War was coming to a close. It was time for Johnson to take on the task of rebuilding a nation.

He opposed the Radical Republican plan for transforming the South. He quickly introduced a more liberal Reconstruction policy. For instance, the new president pardoned, or formally forgave, thousands of former Confederates. He appointed temporary governors to the Southern states and ordered them to organize conventions. At these, delegates, or elected representatives, could draw up new state constitutions and form new governments. Johnson's plan set only a few basic requirements for readmission to the Union. Most important, the former Confederate states had to renounce secession and agree to the abolition of slavery.

Presidential Reconstruction

The years 1865–1867 are often known as Presidential Reconstruction. The Southern states reestablished their governments under President Johnson's generous plan. Former

Confederate leaders dominated the newly elected state legislatures, or lawmaking bodies. These lawmakers quickly restored a society ruled by white supremacy, or the belief that white people are superior to those of other races.

They passed new laws that severely restricted black people's rights and freedoms. These "black codes" included vagrancy laws. These laws meant that unemployed black Americans could be hired out as forced labor as a punishment for unemployment. Other laws made it difficult or impossible for black people to own or rent land. Additionally, many laws made it difficult for them to work at any job other than agricultural laborer or household servant. Slavery had been abolished, but black people were far from free.

The Radical Republican Response

President Johnson's narrow approach to Reconstruction outraged the Radical Republicans. Congress refused to recognize the newly formed Southern governments. Demanding greater protection for the rights of the free black Americans, lawmakers passed several bills designed to bring about real and lasting changes in Southern society. These included the Civil Rights Act of 1866, which extended citizenship to African Americans for the first time. Additionally, these laws included the Reconstruction Acts, which placed the Southern states under military command until the freedmen's rights were guaranteed.

Congress also passed several amendments to the US Constitution to ensure the rights of African Americans. The Fourteenth Amendment defined the basic rights of all citizens, including those that were previously enslaved. Additionally, the Fifteenth Amendment gave the right to vote to all black men. President Johnson opposed all these measures. However, the Republican-controlled Congress passed the bills over his veto, or a rejection of a law or decision.

Ulysses S. Grant was the president of the United States during the bulk of the Reconstruction Era.

Johnson's refusal to compromise on Reconstruction led to increasingly bitter tensions between him and Congress. In 1868, that conflict reached its peak. Congress impeached the president, or charged him with misconduct. After impeachment, only a single vote prevented Johnson's removal from office.

Radical Reconstruction

For the final year of President Johnson's administration and throughout the two terms of President Ulysses S. Grant, the Radical Republicans played a major role in shaping Reconstruction policy. This period is often called Congressional or Radical Reconstruction. The seceded states were divided into districts. The individual districts were headed by US military commanders. These commanders drew up constitutions that granted black men the right to vote and restricted former Confederates from voting or holding political office.

The newly created Southern governments were dominated by Republicans, including black Southerners, white Northerners who moved to the South, and white Southerners who were supporters of Radical Reconstruction. The Reconstruction governments restored and modernized the Southern states. They rebuilt roads and bridges, constructed new railroads, and reorganized the court systems. They also passed laws prohibiting racial discrimination and protecting the rights of black citizens. One of their greatest achievements was the establishment of public school systems throughout the South.

Backlash from White Southerners

Despite these accomplishments, most white Southerners remained bitterly opposed to Reconstruction. During the Grant administration, increasing racial conflicts plagued the South. The anti-Reconstruction Democrats gradually regained control

Rutherford B. Hayes, the nineteenth president of the United States, effectively ended Reconstruction when he withdrew federal troops from the South in 1877.

of Southern state governments. Terrorist groups such as the Ku Klux Klan used intimidation and violence to harass black people and their supporters.

The constant news of race riots, murders carried out by the Klan, government corruption, and election fraud chipped away at Northerners' support for Reconstruction. Northern political leaders became convinced that the only way to restore peace and stability to the South was to leave Southerners to manage their own affairs. In 1877, newly elected president Rutherford B. Hayes withdrew the last federal troops from the South, officially ending Reconstruction.

Over the next few decades, segregation, or the separation of the races, was established throughout the South. African Americans lost many of the rights they had gained through the Reconstruction reforms. It would be nearly a century before a new generation of civil rights activists resumed the struggle for the mission for freedom and equality started under Reconstruction.

President Lincoln delivered the Gettysburg Address in November 1863, on the grounds of one of the bloodiest battles of the Civil War. In it, he called for change for the future of the country.

1 Reunion

By 1863, plans for postwar America were underway even while war still raged on. In January 1863, President Lincoln issued the Emancipation Proclamation. This executive order, or law issued by the president, abolished slavery in all states "in rebellion against the United States." In that same year, he would deliver his famous Gettysburg Address at the cemetery dedication in Pennsylvania. Gettysburg was the site of one of the deadliest battles in the Civil War. In his November speech on the battleground, Lincoln made note of the "great task" that lay ahead. This great task was ending the war and restoring the Union. He was already developing his plan.

Disagreements in the Federal Government

Before the end of the war, Lincoln started forming a plan for returning the eleven seceded states to the Union as quickly and easily as possible. He hoped that a policy of

The Confederate Army would never fully recover from the defeat its troops experienced at the Battle of Gettysburg.

forgiveness and generosity would encourage Southerners to form new governments loyal to the Union.

The Radical Republicans had other ideas. They supported a stricter approach to Reconstruction, with Congress in charge. Their plan aimed to completely transform Southern government and society. In fact, these differences of opinion continued after Lincoln's assassination. Johnson would continue to disagree, more dramatically, with Congress about how the country should move forward.

President Lincoln's Proclamation of Amnesty and Reconstruction

In December 1863, Abraham Lincoln offered a plan of "restoration" to the Southern people. The president's Proclamation of Amnesty and Reconstruction embodied what came to be known as the Ten-Percent Plan. After at least 10 percent of a seceded state's voters took an oath to support the Constitution and the Union, the state could legally establish a new government.

Lincoln's proclamation assumed that the authority for Reconstruction belonged to the president. It offered full amnesty, or forgiveness, to former Confederates who took the loyalty oath.

> Whereas, in and by the Constitution of the United States, it is provided that the President "shall have power to grant reprieves and pardons for offences against the United States, except in cases of impeachment"; and Whereas, a rebellion now exists whereby the loyal state governments of several states have for a long time been subverted, and many persons have committed, and are now guilty of, treason against the United States; ...
>
> Therefore, I, Abraham Lincoln, President of the United States, do proclaim ... to all persons who have, directly or by implication, participated in the existing rebellion ... that a full pardon is hereby granted to them ... with restoration of all rights of property, except as to slaves ... upon the condition that every such person shall take and subscribe an oath ... :
>
> "I, _____, do solemnly swear, in presence of Almighty God, that I will henceforth faithfully support, protect, and defend the Constitution of the United States and the Union of the States thereunder; and that I will, in like manner, abide by and faithfully support all acts of Congress passed during the existing rebellion with reference to slaves ... "
>
> The persons excepted from the benefits of the foregoing provisions are all who are, or shall have

been, civil or diplomatic officers or agents of the so-called Confederate government; ... all who are, or shall have been, military or naval officers of said so-called Confederate government above the rank of colonel in the army or of lieutenant in the navy; [and] all who left seats in the United States Congress to aid the rebellion ...

And I do further proclaim, declare, and make known that whenever, in any of the States of Arkansas, Texas, Louisiana, Mississippi, Tennessee, Alabama, Georgia, Florida, South Carolina, and North Carolina, a number of persons, not less than one tenth in number of the votes cast in such state at the presidential election of the year of our Lord [1860], each having taken the oath, ... shall re-establish a state government ... , such [government] shall be recognized as the true government of the state.

—From Abraham Lincoln's "Proclamation of Amnesty and Reconstruction," December 8, 1863.

CONSIDER THIS

1. What are the three key elements of the loyalty oath?
2. What types of people are excluded from Lincoln's pardon? Why do you think he chose to exclude those groups?

KEY TERMS AND CONCEPTS

From the Abraham Lincoln's Proclamation of Amnesty and Reconstruction:

provision A condition of a legal document.

reprieve A cancelled or postponed punishment.

subverted Undermined the authority of.

From the Wade-Davis Bill:

usurp To seize power.

From the Thirteenth Amendment:

duly Appropriately.

jurisdiction A territory or area that the United States governs.

A Stricter Congressional Policy

Two leaders of the Radical Republicans answered Lincoln's Ten-Percent Plan with a much stricter proposal. Senator Benjamin Wade and Representative Henry Winter Davis proposed the Wade-Davis Bill. This law placed the authority for Reconstruction with Congress, as opposed to with the president.

The bill required that at least 50 percent of a seceded state's voters take the loyalty oath before the state could reestablish its government. The bill also included harsh punishments for former Confederates, including the restrictions outlined in the sections below. Congress passed the Wade-Davis Bill in 1864. However, President Lincoln refused to sign it into law.

Section 4 ... No person who has held or exercised any office, civil or military, state or confederate, under the rebel usurpation, or who has voluntarily borne arms against the United States, shall ... be eligible to be elected as delegate [to a constitutional convention] ...

Section 7 ... The convention shall declare, on behalf of the people of the state, their submission to the constitution and laws of the United States, and shall adopt the following provisions, ... and incorporate them in the constitution of the state, that is to say: First. No person who has held or exercised any office, civil or military, ... under the usurping power, shall vote for or be a member of the legislature, or governor. Second. Involuntary servitude is forever prohibited, and the freedom of all persons is guaranteed ...

Section 14 ... Every person who shall hereafter hold or exercise any office, civil or military, ... in the rebel service, state or confederate, is hereby declared not to be a citizen of the United States.

—From the Wade-Davis Bill, July 8, 1864. Reprinted in Henry Steele Commager, ed., *Documents of American History*, 6th edition (New York: Appleton-Century-Crofts, 1958).

CONSIDER THIS

1. What types of people does the bill punish? What are the forms of punishment?
2. Do you think the punishments are fair and reasonable?

The Thirteenth Amendment

A few months after Lincoln issued the Emancipation Proclamation, Republican senators proposed a constitutional amendment. Constitutional amendments, like the Constitution itself, are laws that make up the fundamental principles of the United States. They are changes or additions to the original Constitution. As of 2018, there are a total of only twenty-seven of these amendments.

Republican senators proposed an amendment to expand emancipation and make sure it would continue after the war's end. In January 1865, Congress passed the Thirteenth Amendment. This amendment officially abolished slavery. The amendment then went to the states for ratification. In order for an amendment to be official, three-fourths of the states must ratify, or officially agree to, the amendment. Under President Lincoln's Reconstruction plan, Southern legislatures were required to approve the amendment before their states could return to the Union.

The Civil War ended in April 1865. In December of that year, the Thirteenth Amendment was finally ratified. It made slavery illegal throughout the United States. However, it would take five more years for all of the seceded states to rejoin the Union. Georgia would be the last in 1870.

SCENE IN THE HOUSE ON THE PASSAGE OF THE PROPOSITION TO AMEND THE CONSTITUTION, JANUARY 31, 1865.

This *Harper's Weekly* illustration depicts how the House of Representatives celebrated after the passage of the Thirteenth Amendment in early 1865.

> Section 1. Neither slavery nor involuntary servitude, except as a punishment for crime whereof the party shall have been duly convicted, shall exist within the United States, or any place subject to their jurisdiction.
>
> Section 2. Congress shall have power to enforce this article by appropriate legislation.
>
> —From the Thirteenth Amendment to the US Constitution (1865). Available at http://www.lawcornell.edu/constitution/constitution.amendmentxiii.html.

CONSIDER THIS

1. Some historians have called the Thirteenth Amendment the most important measure of the nineteenth century. Do you agree?
2. A proposed amendment must be ratified by three-fourths of the states in order to become part of the Constitution. Why do you think the framers of the Constitution made the amendment process so difficult?

Lincoln's Second Inaugural Address

President Lincoln was sworn in for a second term as president in March 1865. Thousands of people gathered in the shadow of the newly completed Capitol dome in Washington, DC. They gathered to hear Lincoln's second inaugural address, or a speech made by an incoming president. In this brief, powerful speech, the president anticipated the war's end in little more than a month and reached out to all Americans.

In March 1865, President Lincoln was inaugurated for the second time. He would only live to see a month of his second term before he was assassinated.

REUNION

Fellow-countrymen: ... On the occasion corresponding to this four years ago all thoughts were anxiously directed to an impending civil war. All dreaded it, all sought to avert it. While the inaugural address was being delivered from this place, devoted altogether to saving the Union without war, urgent agents were in the city seeking to destroy it without war—seeking to dissolve the Union and divide [its] effects by negotiation. Both parties deprecated war, but one of them would make war rather than let the nation survive, and the other would accept war rather than let it perish, and the war came.

One-eighth of the whole population were colored slaves, not distributed generally over the Union, but localized in the southern part of it. These slaves constituted a peculiar and powerful interest. All knew that this interest was somehow the cause of the war. To strengthen, perpetuate, and extend this interest was the object for which the insurgents would rend the Union even by war, while the Government claimed no right to do more than to restrict the territorial enlargement of it. Neither party expected for the war the magnitude or the duration which it has already attained. Neither anticipated that the cause of the conflict might cease with or even before the conflict itself should cease. Each looked for an easier triumph, and a result less fundamental and astounding ... Fondly do we hope, fervently do we pray, that this mighty scourge of war may speedily pass away ...

With malice toward none, with charity for all, with firmness in the right as God gives us to see the right, let us strive on to finish the work we are in, to bind up

KEY TERMS AND CONCEPTS

From President Abraham Lincoln's second inaugural address:

avert To avoid.

colored A dated, now offensive term in the United States, used to refer to black people.

deprecate To strongly disapprove of.

fervently Enthusiastically.

insurgent A rebel, here referring to Southerners who seceded from the Union.

interest In this context, a common concern of a group.

malice Ill will.

perpetuate To preserve.

rend To tear apart.

scourge A troublesome, evil thing.

From President Andrew Johnson's address:

cast ... into oblivion To forget.

elective franchise The right to vote.

suffrage The right to vote.

> the nation's wounds, to care for him who shall have borne the battle and for his widow and his orphan, to do all which may achieve and cherish a just and lasting peace among ourselves and with all nations.
>
> —From Abraham Lincoln's Second Inaugural Address, March 4, 1865.

CONSIDER THIS

1. Who do you think is Lincoln's intended audience?
2. How does the speech reflect his views on Reconstruction?

President Johnson Comments on His Reconstruction Plan

Andrew Johnson was a former Democratic senator from Tennessee. At the time, Democrats were primarily proslavery. Despite the fact that he was a former slave owner from a state that was a part of the Confederate States of America, Johnson had remained loyal to the Union during the Civil War. This earned him the Republican nomination for vice president in the election of 1864.

On April 14, 1865, President Lincoln was shot and fatally wounded at Ford's Theatre in Washington, DC. Following his death, Johnson was sworn in as president. He had different ideas from Lincoln when it came to Reconstruction. The new president believed that "white men alone must manage the South."

Under his moderate Reconstruction plan, provisional, or temporary, governors were appointed to the Southern states. These governors were required to call constitutional conventions, where white Southern representatives could draft new state constitutions. The newly established state governments were required to renounce secession and ratify the Thirteenth Amendment, abolishing slavery.

No other measures protecting the rights of formerly enslaved people were required.

By the end of 1865, Johnson had officially recognized the new governments of nearly all of the former Confederate states. In his year-end address to Congress, he reviewed his actions during his early months as president.

> Provisional governors have been appointed for the States, conventions called, governors elected, legislatures assembled, and Senators and Representatives chosen to the Congress of the United States ...
>
> The next step which I have taken to restore the constitutional relations of the States has been an invitation to them to participate in the high office of amending the Constitution ... On the one side the plan of restoration shall proceed in conformity with a willingness to cast the disorders of the past into oblivion, and ... on the other the evidence of sincerity in the future maintenance of the Union shall be put beyond any doubt by the ratification of the proposed amendment to the Constitution, which provides for the abolition of slavery forever within the limits of our country ...
>
> Every danger of conflict is avoided when the settlement of the question [of black suffrage] is referred to the several States. They can, each for itself, decide on the measure, and whether it is to be adopted at once and absolutely or introduced gradually and with conditions. In my judgment the freedmen, if they show patience and manly virtues, will sooner obtain a participation in the

> elective franchise through the States than through the General Government, even if it had power to intervene. When the tumult of emotions that have been raised by the suddenness of the social change shall have subsided, it may prove that they will receive the kindest usage from some of those on whom they have heretofore most closely depended.
>
> —From Andrew Johnson's First Annual Message to Congress, December 4, 1865. Reprinted in James D. Richardson, ed., A *Compilation of the Messages and Papers of the Presidents,* Volume VI (Washington, DC: US Government Printing Office, 1897).

CONSIDER THIS

1. How does Johnson's speech reveal his most important concerns in dealing with the former Confederate states?
2. What is his policy regarding the voting rights of black people? How do you think the freedmen reacted to his statements on this issue?

The Problem with States' Rights

President Johnson left a lot of power with the states. This is because of the Tenth Amendment to the Constitution, ratified in 1791. The amendment says that all decisions not outlined by the Constitution are up to the states to decided. This idea is usually referred to as states' rights.

With states' rights in place, Johnson left many of the decisions about how to rebuild the South up to white Southerners. As you can imagine, these former slaveholders did not always create laws that were fair to the black people living under their rule.

This 1874 *Harper's Weekly* political cartoon suggests that white supremacy groups made life more difficult for African Americans than slavery did.

2

Discrimination and Disenfranchisement

The Southern state governments established under President Johnson's Reconstruction plan were dominated by former Confederate leaders. Southern legislatures quickly passed a series of laws to restore white control over formerly enslaved black people. These "black codes" sharply limited the black people's rights and freedoms. They helped ensure that African Americans would continue to serve as laborers for white employers.

Disenfranchisement

In addition to creating these laws restricting what black people could and could not do, many states did not give black people the right to vote. This concept is called disenfranchisement. Because the freedmen could not vote, white Southerners were able to continue electing other white Southerners to office. These officials often protected white Southern interests, which included restricting black people's rights. Despite the commonness of these systems of Southern governance, there were many who found these policies problematic.

Frederick Douglass Discusses Voting Rights

Frederick Douglass was a leading spokesperson for African American rights before, during, and after the Civil War. Douglass was born enslaved, but he escaped to freedom as a young man.

Frederick Douglass was an active abolitionist and intellectual who spoke out about emancipation and enfranchisement.

KEY TERMS AND CONCEPTS

From Frederick Douglass's speech:

enfranchisement The act of giving someone the right to vote.

As an adult, he gained fame as an abolitionist lecturer, writer, and newspaper publisher.

He delivered the following message in a speech to the Massachusetts Anti-Slavery Society. In this speech, delivered a few days before the war's end, he explained the significance of enfranchisement, or the right to vote, for the freed slaves.

> ... I am for the "immediate, unconditional and universal" enfranchisement of the black man, in every State ... Without this, his liberty is a mockery; without this, you might as well almost retain the old name of slavery for his condition; for ... he is the slave of society ...
>
> —Frederick Douglass, "What the Black Man Wants," April 1865. Reprinted in Philip S. Foner, ed., *The Life and Writings of Frederick Douglass* (New York: International Publishers Company, 1976).

CONSIDER THIS

1. What arguments does Douglass use to support his demand for black enfranchisement?

An Appeal to Congress

As the Civil War drew to a close, and after it was over, people who were formerly enslaved joined together in conventions to discuss ways to safeguard their hard-won liberty. The Convention of Colored Citizens of the State of Virginia held one of these meetings in Alexandria, Virginia, in August 1865. It drew thousands of freedmen as well as abolitionists.

After four days of speeches and discussions, the delegates of the convention made an appeal to Congress. They were seeking enfranchisement. In the appeal, the representatives discussed how many of these black men served the government as soldiers in the Civil War but now were under the control of corrupt Southerners. These Southerners claimed they were loyal to the Union, but they only cared about serving their own interests.

> We know these men ... We assure you that ... loyalty is ... used as a cover to the ... design of getting restored to their former relations with the ... Government, and ... to render the freedom you have given us more intolerable than the slavery they intended for us ...
>
> —From "Address to the Loyal Citizens and Congress of the United States of America," Proceedings of the Convention of the Colored People of Virginia, Held in the City of Alexandria, August 2–5, 1865, Alexandria, VA, 1865. Reprinted in Richard N. Current, ed., *Reconstruction, 1865–1877* (Englewood Cliffs, NJ: Prentice-Hall, 1965).

This 1867 image depicts a black man casting his vote in Virginia. Many African Americans, however, were not able to cast their votes because of laws, restrictions, and intimidation, even after the Fifteenth Amendment was ratified in 1870, guaranteeing African American men the right to vote.

CONSIDER THIS

1. What do the freedmen fear?
2. How do you think they expected voting rights to protect them from white Southerners?

Mississippi's Black Codes

Despite the fact that freedmen and abolitionists were working to secure rights for black people, other forces were at work. States enforced laws that restricted different aspects of life for the newly freed. For instance, in 1865, the Mississippi state legislature passed a series of these laws, called black codes.

The following three excerpts are examples of such laws. The first enforces labor laws requiring a legal contract that bound freedmen to their employers.

> Section 6. All contracts for labor made with freedmen, free Negroes, and mulattoes … shall be in writing … and if the laborer shall quit the service of the employer before the expiration of his term of service, without good cause, he shall forfeit his wages for that year.
>
> Section 7. … Every civil officer shall, and every person may, arrest and carry back to his or her legal employer any freedman, free negro, or mulatto who shall have quit the service of his or her employer before the expiration of his or her term of service without good cause.
>
> —From "The Black Codes of Mississippi 1865." Reprinted in Henry Steele Commager, ed., *Documents of American History*, 6th edition (New York: Appleton-Century-Crofts, 1958)

The second deals with forced apprenticeships of freed children who were orphans or who did not have parents who could support them.

> Section 1. … It shall be the duty of all sheriffs, justices of the peace, and other civil officers … to report … all freedmen, free negroes, and mulattoes, under the age of eighteen, … who are orphans, or whose parent or parents have not the means or who refuse to provide for and support said minors; and thereupon it shall be the duty of [the] court to apprentice said minors to some competent and suitable person, on such terms as the court may direct …
>
> Section 3. … In the management and control of said apprentice, said master or mistress shall have the power to inflict such moderate corporeal chastisement as a father or guardian is allowed to inflict on his or her child …
>
> Section 4. … If any apprentice shall leave the employment of his or her master or mistress, without his or her consent, said master or mistress may pursue and recapture said apprentice.
>
> —From "The Black Codes of Mississippi 1865." Reprinted in Henry Steele Commager, ed., *Documents of American History*, 6th edition (New York: Appleton-Century-Crofts, 1958).

KEY TERMS AND CONCEPTS

From "The Black Codes of Mississippi 1865":
corporeal chastisement Physical punishment.
mulattoes A now dated term to refer to people of mixed black and white ancestry.

From Richard Somer's account:
vestige A trace.

The third allows adults to be imprisoned or fined for not having suitable employment.

> Section 2. ... All freedmen, free negroes, and mulattoes in this State, over the age of eighteen years, found ... with no lawful employment or business, or found unlawfully assembling themselves together either in the day or nighttime, ... shall be deemed vagrants, and, on conviction thereof shall be fined ... and imprisoned.
>
> —From "The Black Codes of Mississippi 1865." Reprinted in Henry Steele Commager, ed., *Documents of American History*, 6th edition (New York: Appleton-Century-Crofts, 1958).

CONSIDER THIS

1. In what ways did Mississippi's laws violate the rights of black Americans?
2. How did the black codes benefit white employers?

The Devastated South

While people in the federal government argued about how to enforce a realistic plan and state governments enforced unfair laws, the people in the South suffered. After the Civil War, the South was in poverty and ruins. Newly freed enslaved Africans and white Southerners were both displaced by war and destruction. Uniquely hindered, however, were black people who did not know much beyond their former plantations.

Northerner Richard Somers traveled through Alabama's Tennessee River valley during the years that followed the war. He described the dilemma of plantation owners and the newly freed Africans.

> The trail of war is visible throughout the valley in burnt-up gin-houses, ruined bridges, mills, and factories, and in large tracts of once cultivated lands stripped of every vestige of fencing ... The roads, long neglected, are in disorder, and having in many places become impassable, new tracks have been made through the woods and fields without much respect to boundaries. Borne down by losses, debts, and accumulating taxes, many who were once the richest among their fellows have disappeared from the scene, and few have yet

Much of Richmond was in ruins after the end of the Civil War. The South literally needed to be rebuilt after all of the damage.

risen to take their places ... When the war ended, and the bond of slavery was dissolved, ... swarms [of freedmen] went off to seek new masters in the field of free labour, and after a season of trials, often bitter, are only returning by degrees to their old homes ... I have seen more than one great plantation absolutely deserted, ... void of fence or labour.

—From Robert Somers, *The Southern States Since the War: 1870–1* (New York: Macmillan, 1871).

CONSIDER THIS

1. What signs of the war's impact did the writer observe?
2. Why do you think the freedmen returned to the plantations?

Congress Steps In

Despite the fact that states' rights allowed for state governments to create laws that disenfranchised and mistreated black people, the federal government tried to truly rebuild. One month before the end of the Civil War, Congress established the Bureau of Refugees, Freedmen, and Abandoned Lands. Although the organization was commonly known as the Freedmen's Bureau, it was dedicated to helping white and black Southerners alike.

The Freedmen's Bureau opened schools all over the South, like this one in South Carolina.

3

The Bureau of Refugees, Freedmen, and Abandoned Lands

The Freedmen's Bureau was a temporary agency. The government set it up to operate for one year under the administration of the War Department, but it was renewed for several years. At the bureau's peak of operations, it only had about nine hundred agents. Nevertheless, the bureau had an important mission, to provide support for the nearly four million people who had been freed from slavery. It also aimed to provide aid and services to white Southerners who had been left poor and homeless by the Civil War. The bureau supported fifteen states in addition to the District of Columbia in attempting to rebuild after the war. In total, the agency was operational from 1865 until 1872.

The Basics of the Bureau

The bureau was one of the measures put into place in hopes of rebuilding the South after the war. The appointed bureau officials provided food, clothing, and medical care to needy Southerners, both black and white. In the first year, the bureau distributed 150,000 daily food rations, or a fixed amount of food given on a regular basis, to refugees and freedmen in Tennessee and Kentucky alone.

Over time, however, most of the bureau's services benefited people who were previously enslaved. Those special services included helping black communities establish churches and schools. Additionally, the officials supervised labor relations and contracts between former slaves and masters. They also tried to protect the freedmen from mistreatment and violence.

At first, the Freedmen's Bureau had no trouble raising funds to fulfill its many duties. Congress gave the new agency the authority to take over lands and property abandoned by plantation owners who fled from Union troops. Some of the confiscated lands were sold to pay for bureau operations. Other plots were rented to freedmen, often in return for a share of their crops.

All across the South, landless black families were thrilled by rumors that the government planned to give every former slave "forty acres and a mule." (Forty acres is the equivalent of about 16 hectares.) These were supposed to serve as reparations, or compensation for wrongdoings. In early 1866, however, those hopes were dashed. President Johnson returned all confiscated lands to their pre–Civil War owners. Johnson's actions not only shattered the freedmen's dreams of land ownership. His decisions also eliminated the main source of funding for the Freedmen's Bureau.

Praise for a Job Well Done

During the Reconstruction period, *Harper's Weekly* was America's leading magazine of social and political commentary. The magazine's news columns, strongly worded editorials, and political cartoons gave it a distinctive voice that both reflected and helped shape public opinion. *Harper's Weekly* was a strong supporter of Radical Reconstruction and the Freedmen's Bureau. For instance, the magazine published a cartoon by Alfred R. Waud, shown on page 54, that honored the work the Freedmen's Bureau had done.

The Dismantling of the Bureau

Although the agency was only supposed to be in existence for a year, Congress voted twice to extend the Freedmen's Bureau. However, most bureau operations were discontinued in January 1869. In 1872, the agency was completely terminated. Unfortunately, a lack of funding and opposition from conservatives in both the North and the South prevented bureau officials from accomplishing many of their ambitious goals. Despite these obstacles, however, the Freedmen's Bureau did help millions of people affected by the war.

The Freedmen's Bureau Act

The Freedmen's Bureau was the first federal agency to provide social welfare, or government aid to support public health and happiness, to Americans. Congress passed the act establishing the bureau on March 3, 1865. The Freedmen's Bureau Act detailed the new agency's three-part mission. First, the bureau was responsible for providing social services to freed slaves and white refugees. Second, it was supposed to take control of Confederate lands that

This Alfred R. Waud political cartoon depicts how the Freedmen's Bureau worked to diffuse tension between white and black people.

had been seized by the Union army. Lastly, they were responsible for giving out the confiscated lands to the freedmen. The following excerpt is a portion of the act.

> Be it enacted by the Senate and House of Representatives of the United States of America in Congress assembled, That there is hereby established in the War Department, to continue during the present war of rebellion, and for one year thereafter, a bureau of refugees, freedmen, and abandoned lands, to which shall be committed ... the supervision and management of all abandoned lands, and the control of all subjects relating to refugees and freedmen from rebel states ... The said bureau shall be under the management and control of a commissioner to be

appointed by the President, by and with the advice and consent of the Senate …

Section 2. … The Secretary of War may direct such issues of provisions, clothing, and fuel, as he may deem needful for the immediate and temporary shelter and supply of destitute and suffering refugees and freedmen and their wives and children …

Section 4. … The commissioner, under the direction of the President, shall have authority to set apart, for the use of loyal refugees and freedmen, such tracts of land within the insurrectionary states as shall have been abandoned, or to which the United States shall have acquired title by confiscation or sale, or otherwise, and to every male citizen, whether refugee or freedman . . . there shall be assigned not more than forty acres of such land, and the person to whom it was so assigned shall be protected in the use and enjoyment of the land for the term of three years … At the end of said term, or at any time during said term, the occupants of any parcels so assigned may purchase the land.

—From "An Act to Establish a Bureau for the Relief of Freedmen and Refugees," March 3, 1865.

CONSIDER THIS

1. What could freedmen and refugees expect to receive from the Freedmen's Bureau?
2. Why do you think land ownership was so important to those that were previously enslaved?

KEY TERMS AND CONCEPTS

From the Freedmen's Bureau Act:

destitute The condition of being without means for survival.

enacted Made into law.

insurrectionary states States that rose up against the government.

parcel A piece of land.

From Colonel Eliphalet Whittlesey's account:

besieged Surrounded in large numbers.

depot A storage facility.

hovel and shanty Small, poorly constructed buildings.

idle Lazy.

insolent Disrespectful.

From M. H. Puckett's account:

armed to the hilt Heavily armed with weapons.

Bushwhackers Confederate rebels.

desperadoes Reckless people or criminals.

remuneration Money earned for work completed.

thwart To prevent from happening.

THE BUREAU OF REFUGEES, FREEDMEN, AND ABANDONED LANDS

An Assistant Commissioner's Account

Union army general Oliver Otis Howard was appointed commissioner, or selected as the authority figure, of the Freedmen's Bureau. Assistant commissioners were assigned to each of the Southern states. Colonel Eliphalet Whittlesey was assistant commissioner for North Carolina. In this report, he describes the conditions he found on his arrival in the state capital, Raleigh.

> On the 22d of June I arrived at Raleigh with instructions ... to take control of all subjects relating to "refugees, freedmen, and the abandoned lands" within this State. I found these subjects in much confusion. Hundreds of white refugees and thousands of blacks were collected about this and other towns, occupying every hovel and shanty, living upon government [food] rations, without employment and without comfort, many dying for want of proper food and medical supplies. A much larger number, both white and black, were crowding into the towns, and literally swarming about every depot of supplies to receive their rations ... The street in front of the post's commissary's office was blocked up with vehicles of all the descriptions peculiar to North Carolina, and with people who had come from the country around ... for government rations. These were destitute whites, and were supplied by order of the department commander. Our own headquarters, and every office of the bureau, was besieged from morning till night by freedmen, some coming many miles on foot, others in wagons and carts. The rations issued would scarcely last till they reached home ...

I have made every effort to protect them [the freedmen] from wrong. Suddenly set free, they were at first exhilarated by the air of liberty, and committed some excesses. To be sure of their freedom, many thought they must leave the old scenes of oppression and seek new homes. Others regarded the property accumulated by their labor as in part their own, and demanded a share of it. On the other hand, the former masters, suddenly stripped of their wealth, at first looked upon the freedmen with a mixture of hate and fear. In these circumstances some collisions were inevitable. The negroes were complained of as idle, insolent, and dishonest; while they complained that they were treated more cruelly than when they were slaves ... All officers of the bureau were directed ... to investigate these difficulties between the two classes, to settle them ... as far as possible, to punish light offences by fines or otherwise, and to report more serious cases of crime to the military authorities for trial.

—From "Freedmen's Bureau Report, North Carolina, 1865" in *Report of the Joint Committee on Reconstruction of the First Session Thirty-Ninth Congress* (Washington, DC: US Government Printing Office, 1866).

CONSIDER THIS

1. According to the commissioner, what were the most pressing problems in Raleigh?
2. What beliefs and attitudes caused conflicts between former masters and former slaves?

Tennessee Official M. H. Puckett's Report

Many Southern whites were angry and frustrated after the war. They lashed out at black people. The Freedmen's Bureau was charged with investigating and punishing all such violent attacks. In this letter, a bureau official expresses his frustration about the "outrages" committed in his district in Tennessee.

> January 15, 1866 ...
>
> Since April 15 [1865] there have been numerous outrages committed against freedmen in this district. The violence committed was generally death ... During the rebellion the freedman was kept under the control of their rebel master by violence for if any left their former master they sent the young bands of Bushwhackers after him and when [he] was found he was deliberately shot down. This deterred many from leaving and this today keeps them from getting remuneration for their work ...
>
> There is still lingering in this county a set of desperadoes that have never yet submitted to the civil authorities, armed to the hilt, who are still the terror to the freedmen, urged up no doubt by the citizens here. It so happened that a freedman had done some work for a bar keeper in Vernon in this county for which he applied for a settlement and while in the house 3 of them outlaws entered and commenced up on the Black man, all to abuse him, first with words. The freedman made no resistance and started to leave whereupon they drew their side arms and deliberately presented at his head. Fortunately it

failed fire, whereupon [an outlaw] seized a butcher knife and ran after him, the Negro being the strongest seized him and threw him to the ground and held him until some one interfered and made a settlement of the difficulty as all through. But he was no sooner released when [another man] gathered an axe and made after him again, this time the Negro ran some 2 or three hundred yards and kept out of the way ... When he got him back [they] commenced the 3rd time with bricks and rocks, succeeded in striking him several times, bruising him up severely. I attempted to have this matter thoroughly investigated but could get nobody or persons to arrest the parties. I even tried the Military who also refuse ...

There is every disposition that can be conceived of to thwart the workings of the Bureau. If anything is wrong on the part of the freedman I must do something and when I attempt to right it every conceivable obstacle is thrown in my way.

M. H. Puckett ...
Hickman County Tenn.

—From "Report of Outrages, Riots and Murders, Jan. 15, 1866–Aug. 12, 1868" (National Archives Microfilm Publication M999, Roll 34).

CONSIDER THIS

1. What does the official believe is behind the attacks on the freedmen?
2. What problems does he face in trying to do his job?

The Case of "Freedman Dan"

One important area of Freedmen's Bureau operations involved family services. The agency provided information and assistance to unite the families of former slaves. It also helped relocate hundreds of thousands of people left stranded by the war. In this letter, a bureau officer in South Carolina arranges transportation for a freedman left all alone in Charleston.

> [August 1866]
> Lt. Col. H. W. Smith ...
> Charleston, S.C.
>
> Colonel,
> I have the honor to request that transportation may be furnished for the destitute freed-man Dan from this place to Newberry, S.C. He was brought here by his owners some two years ago to prevent his falling into the hands of our forces and has been left here by them. He is almost blind and can do no work. His connections live at Newberry and have sent for him to go to them, they promising to provide for him. There will in all probability be a scarcity of provisions here next year and unless this man can be sent to his family he must become a charge to this Bureau ...
>
> your Obedt. [Obedient] Servant
> William Stone
>
> —From "Records of the Assistant Commissioner for the State of South Carolina" (National Archives Publication M869, Roll 44).

CONSIDER THIS

1. How did Dan become stranded in South Carolina?
2. How do you think his relatives might have learned of his location?

Harriet Norwood's Labor Contract

Former slave owners often tried to trick former slaves into working for them under terms that weren't much different from the old slavery system. The Freedmen's Bureau protected these workers by drawing up fair labor contracts that spelled out the terms of employment. These contracts outlined work responsibilities, wages, and benefits such as lodging, food, clothing, and medical care.

Bureau officials also drew up agreements of indenture, or apprenticeship, for orphans and children whose parents could not provide for them. These contracts bound a child to work for an employer for a specified period of time in return for food, lodging, and instruction in a trade. In the following indenture agreement, Freedmen's Bureau official Fred W. Thibaut acts as guardian for nine-year-old Harriet Norwood. She becomes an apprentice to William G. John.

> To all whom it may concern
> Greeting:
>
> This indenture made and entered into on this tenth day of October in the year of our Lord One Thousand Eight Hundred and Sixty Seven at Washington in the County of Hempstead in the state of Arkansas by and between Fred W. Thibaut ..., Superintendent of Freedmen's, Refugees, etc, and ... guardian of one Harriet Norwood, a freed girl, an orphan minor

having no estate for her maintenance and education, aged nine years, and William G. John …

The said Fred W. Thibaut … does hereby put, place and bind out the said Harriet Norwood … to the said William G. John to learn the art of housekeeping, cooking, washing, ironing and sewing from the date hereof until Harriet Norwood shall arrive at the age of eighteen years—during all of which time the said Harriet Norwood shall well and faithfully serve the said William G. John, and everywhere and at all times obey his lawful commands … She shall not contract matrimony during the period for which she is hereby apprenticed without the knowledge and consent of said John. She shall not absent herself from the service of said John; but shall in all things and at all times behave and conduct herself as a good and faithful apprentice ought to do …

And the said William G. John on his part does hereby covenant, promise and agree, to teach and instruct the said Harriet Norwood … in the art or business of housekeeping, cooking, washing, ironing and sewing; to well and faithfully provide for the said apprentice sufficient meat, drink, clothing, lodging and all other necessaries …

And the said William G. John does hereby further covenant and bind himself to teach said apprentice or cause her to be taught reading, writing, and arithmetic.

—From "Indentures of Apprenticeship Dec. 1865–Feb. 1868, Contracts: Jan. 1, 1865–Jan. 1, 1868" (National Archives Microfilm Publication M999, Roll 20).

CONSIDER THIS

1. What are the benefits to both parties in this apprenticeship arrangement?
2. Who do you think benefits most?

Edmonia Highgate's Experience in Louisiana

Under the slave laws, it was illegal to teach a slave to read and write. When the first schools for freed slaves opened after the Civil War, they were crowded with eager students—adults and children alike. Most freedmen's schools were founded and operated by Northern charities or by Southern black men and women who had been secretly educated. The Freedmen's Bureau helped by supervising the new schools, renting buildings for classrooms, contributing funds for books and other supplies, and paying for the transportation of teachers. The bureau also provided military protection for students and teachers against those white Southerners who violently opposed black education.

In the following letter, teacher Edmonia Highgate describes interactions between eager students and hostile townspeople in Louisiana. Highgate was the daughter of freed slaves living in New York. She had traveled south near the war's end to establish freedmen's schools on behalf of a Christian charity.

December 17th, 1866

Dear Friend:

Perhaps you may care to know of my work here for the Freed people ... I have a very interesting

Schools built by the Freedmen's Bureau were often terrorized. Many were burned down by hostile white Southerners.

and constantly growing day school, a night school, and, a glorious Sabbath School of near one hundred scholars. The school is under the auspices of the Freedman's Bureau, yet it is wholly self-supporting. The majority of my pupils come from plantations, three, four and even eight miles distant [5 to 13 kilometers]. So anxious are they to learn that they walk these distances so early in the morning as never to be tardy. Every scholar buys his own book and [writing] slate, etc. ... They, with but few exceptions are french Creoles. My little knowledge of French is just to instruct them in our language. They do learn rapidly. A class who did not understand any English came to school last Monday morning and at the close of the week they were reading "Easy Lessons" ... Most of the men, women and large children are hired by the year "on contract" upon the plantations of their former so called masters. One of the articles of agreement is that the planter shall pay "a five percent tax for the education of the children of his laborers." ...

There is more than work for two teachers yet I am all alone, God has wonderously spared me. There has been much opposition to the School. Twice I have been shot at in my room. Some of my night-school scholars have been shot but none killed. A week ago an aged freedman was shot so badly as to break his arm and leg—just across the way. The rebels here threatened to burn down the school and house in which I board before the first month was passed. Yet they have not materially harmed us. The nearest military Jurisdiction is two hundred miles [320 km] distant at New Orleans ...

Yours for Christ's poor,
Edmonia G. Highgate

—From Amistad Research Center, American Missionary Association Archives, Tulane University, New Orleans, Louisiana.

KEY TERMS AND CONCEPTS

From Edmonia Highgate's letter:

auspices Control.

French Creole A person of mixed French and African descent.

jurisdiction Legal authority.

just Enough.

From James D. B. DeBow's congressional testimony:

reconciled Settled or resolved, as with a dispute.

CONSIDER THIS

1. What were some of the challenges Highgate faced as a teacher in a freedmen's school?
2. What hardships did the students endure to get an education?

A Southerner Advises Against Interference

White Southerners disliked the "interference," or involvement, of the federal agents of the Freedmen's Bureau. James D. B. DeBow was a magazine editor in New Orleans. He presented his opinions concerning the Freedmen's Bureau in front of a congressional committee investigating the conditions in the South. He expressed a view held by many Southerners. He believed if the North would just leave Southerners alone, then they could easily work out their problems.

question: What is your opinion of the necessity or utility of the Freedmen's Bureau? ...

answer: I think if the whole regulation of the negroes, or freedmen, were left to the people of the communities in which they live, it will be administered for the best interest of the negroes as well as of the white men. I think there is a kindly feeling on the part of the planters towards the freedmen. They are not held at all responsible for anything that has happened. They are looked upon as the innocent cause. In talking with a number of planters, I remember some of them telling me they were succeeding very well with their freedmen, having got a preacher to preach to them and a teacher to teach to them, believing it was for the interest of the planter to make the negro feel reconciled; for, to lose his services as a laborer for even a few months would be very disastrous ... Leave the people to themselves, and they will manage very well. The Freedmen's Bureau, or any agency to interfere between the freedman and his former master, is only productive of mischief.

—From the testimony of James D. B. DeBow before the Joint Committee on Reconstruction, March 28, 1866, in *Report of the Joint Committee on Reconstruction of the First Session Thirty-Ninth Congress* (Washington, DC: US Government Printing Office, 1866).

CONSIDER THIS

1. What does DeBow's testimony reveal about his attitude toward black people?
2. What argument does he use to explain why former masters would, if left to their own devices, treat the freedmen fairly?
3. How do you think a former slave might have responded to DeBow's comments?

Congress Versus the President

Despite the positive contributions of the Freedmen's Bureau, there were always forces at work against them. Congress, the governing body responsible for the bureau, had to fight against violent and frustrated Southerners. They were up against opinions like DeBow's. Additionally, they were ultimately up against the president of the United States. During the early Reconstruction years, Johnson and Congress found themselves going head to head on issues that affected rebuilding the nation.

Under President Andrew Johnson's Reconstruction plan, many former Confederate leaders regained control of Southern state governments. Southern legislatures quickly passed discriminatory black codes and elected former Confederates to the US Senate. Johnson's plan meant that former plantation owners and those with mindsets responsible for the Civil War found themselves in positions of power again.

This situation frustrated the Republicans in Congress. Moderate, or not radical, Republicans worried that Johnson's policies seemed to be rewarding old enemies and restoring rebel governments. Meanwhile, Radical Republicans denounced the president's actions as "madness."

LEGISLATIVE

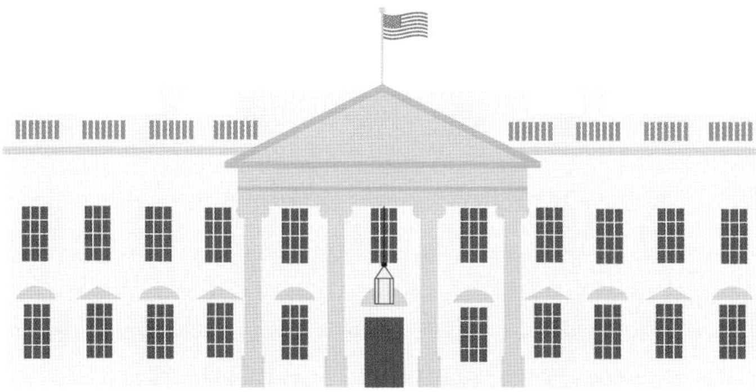

EXECUTIVE

JUDICIAL

Together, the judicial, legislative, and executive branches make up the US government. Although they work together, they do not always agree.

4

The Executive and Legislative Clash

There are three branches of the US government: the legislative, executive, and judicial branches. The legislative branch is Congress, made up of the Senate and the House of Representatives. It is responsible for creating laws. The executive branch is made up of the president, vice president, and the president's cabinet. It is responsible for enforcing and carrying out laws. The judicial branch is made up of the Supreme Court and other federal courts. It is responsible for interpreting laws. Usually, these three branches of government work together to run the nation. During Reconstruction, however, the legislative and executive branches were at odds.

Congress Fights Back

Congress took its first steps to oppose Presidential Reconstruction in December 1865. Returning from a long recess, the lawmakers refused to recognize the new

Southern state governments or admit their newly elected senators. Then they began to draft a series of proposed laws designed to protect black people. One by one the president vetoed, or formally rejected, the bills. One by one Congress passed these laws despite Johnson's vetoes. Congress can override, or undo, a president's veto if a bill is approved by a two-thirds majority in both the House and the Senate.

Johnson's stubborn refusal to compromise on Reconstruction gradually pushed many conservative and moderate Republicans into the Radical camp. For his part, the president denounced Congress's actions. He did everything in his power to prevent enforcement of the antidiscrimination laws.

Johnson's Impeachment

In 1868, the increasingly bitter struggle between the president and Congress came to a head. On February 24, 1868, the House of Representatives successfully voted to impeach Johnson. It was the first attempt to impeach a president in US history. On March 5, the Senate trial, addressing the charges the House filed against the president, began. Two-thirds of the senators needed to vote to remove him from office. On May 16, Johnson was saved from removal by a single vote. Thirty-five of the fifty-four senators voted to remove him, while nineteen voted to acquit, or find him not guilty, of his crimes.

While the president's opponents were unsuccessful in their attempt to remove him from office, they succeeded in stripping Johnson of power. For the remainder of Johnson's administration, Congress controlled the Reconstruction efforts.

Thaddeus Stevens Calls for an Overhaul of the South

In December 1865, Republican lawmakers returned from recess determined to unravel President Johnson's Reconstruction policies. A committee of fifteen senators and representatives was formed

Congressman Thaddeus Stevens, a leader of the Radical Republicans, rejected President Johnson's Reconstruction policies.

to develop an alternate congressional plan. It was called the Joint Committee on Reconstruction. It was responsible for drafting the charges against Johnson.

One of the most outspoken members of the Joint Committee on Reconstruction was Thaddeus Stevens. He was a representative from Pennsylvania and a leader of the Radical Republicans. Stevens believed that the Southern states should not be readmitted to the Union until they gave the freedmen land and the right to vote. In a speech delivered in his hometown of Lancaster, the lawmaker advocated strict federal control of the South. He hoped this control would help change Southern society and its institutions.

> The armies of the Confederate states having been conquered and subdued, and their territory possessed by the United States, it becomes necessary to establish governments therein which shall be republican in form and principles and form a more "perfect Union" with the parent government. It is desirable that such a course should be pursued as to exclude from those governments every vestige of human bondage, and render the same impossible in this nation ...
>
> We hold it to be the duty of government to inflict condign punishment on the rebel belligerents, and so weaken their hands that they can never again endanger the Union; and so reform their municipal institutions as to make them republican in spirit as well as in name.
>
> We especially insist that the property of the chief rebels should be seized ...

There are about six millions of freedmen in the South ... By thus [confiscating] the estates of the leading rebels, the government would have 394,000,000 of acres [160 million hectares] ... Divide this land into convenient farms. Give, if you please, forty acres to each adult male freedman ... This plan would, no doubt, work a radical reorganization in Southern institutions, habits and manners. It is intended to revolutionize their principles and feelings ...The whole fabric of southern society must be changed, and never can it be done if this opportunity is lost ...

If the South is ever to be made a safe Republic, let her lands be cultivated by the toil of the owners, or the free labor of intelligent citizens. This must be done even though it drive her nobility into exile. If they go, all the better ... It is far easier and more beneficial to exile 70,000 proud, bloated and defiant rebels, than to expatriate four millions of laborers, native to the soil and loyal to the Government.

—From Thaddeus Stevens's speech in Lancaster, Pennsylvania, September 6, 1865.

CONSIDER THIS

1. What words convey Stevens's feelings about the former Confederates?
2. Do you think the freedmen were entitled to the land of former plantation owners?

KEY TERMS AND CONCEPTS

From Thaddeus Stevens's speech:

condign Appropriate or fitting.

expatriate To remove from the country. In nineteenth-century America, some advocated for expatriating former slaves by transporting them to Africa.

municipal Relating to cities or towns.

reform To change.

subdued Overpowered or brought under control.

toil Hard manual labor.

The Civil Rights Act of 1866

The first major piece of Radical Republican legislation was the Civil Rights Act of 1866. The law worked against the discriminatory black codes. It extended the rights of citizenship to all black Americans, whether they had been born enslaved or free.

In one sense, this was a dramatic break with the past. In 1857, the Supreme Court ruled quite the opposite in the controversial *Dred Scott* case. In said case, an enslaved man named Dred Scott sued for his freedom. The Supreme Court decided, however, that Scott had no grounds to sue because, being black, he was not a citizen. The Civil Rights Act, however, was in direct opposition to the Supreme Court's decision.

At the same time, the law was considered a moderate measure. Although it granted black people citizenship, it still did not give African Americans the right to vote or to sit on juries.

Be it enacted, That all persons born in the United States and not subject to any foreign power, excluding Indians not taxed, are hereby declared to be citizens of the United States; and such citizens, of every race and color, without regard to any previous condition of slavery or involuntary servitude, except as punishment for crime whereof the party shall have been duly convicted, shall have the same right, in every State and Territory in the United States, to make and enforce contracts, to sue, be parties [to lawsuits], and give evidence, to inherit, purchase, lease, sell, hold, and convey real and personal property, and to full and equal benefit of all laws and proceedings for the security of person and property, as is enjoyed by white citizens, and shall be subject to like punishment, pains, and penalties, and to none other, any law, statute, ordinance, regulation, or custom to the contrary.

—From the Civil Rights Act of 1866. Reprinted in Henry Steele Commager, ed., *Documents of American History*, 6th edition (New York: Appleton-Century-Crofts, 1958).

CONSIDER THIS

1. How does the Civil Rights Act define the basic rights of all American citizens?
2. How does it take the authority to grant citizenship away from the states and give it to the federal government alone?

Harper's Weekly Responds to President Johnson

Congress passed the Civil Rights Act on March 13, 1866. Two weeks later, President Johnson vetoed it. He declared that the black people were not ready for the privileges and responsibilities of citizenship. Johnson also argued that the legislation was unconstitutional because it interfered with the rights of state governments. He was referring to states' rights and the Tenth Amendment.

Harper's Weekly responded to Johnson's frustrations with this editorial. It defended the federal government's authority to establish the citizenship of the freedmen. On April 9, the Civil Rights Act became law when Congress passed it over the president's veto.

> The Civil Rights Bill was drawn with simplicity and care for a very necessary purpose. It declares who are citizens of the United States, defines their rights, prescribes penalties for violating them, and provides means of redress ...
>
> It is certainly essential ... that the true meaning of citizenship should be defined. Nearly a fifth of the population of the country are colored ... They are native to the soil. They owe and perform the obligations of other citizens. Why not call them citizens? ...
>
> The Dred Scott decision declared that a free negro was not a citizen. In 1862, under the Government purged of the influence of slavery, the question again arose, and [the government] ... held that color was not a disqualification. But the baffled party of disunion [the Democrats] still asserts the contrary.

President Johnson in his veto of the Civil Rights Bill admits a difference of opinion; and the Constitution, while it speaks of citizens, nowhere defines the term. It is therefore both timely and wise, at the close of a civil war which has abolished slavery, that the highest authority should declare distinctly who are citizens of the United States, and what are the rights to which citizens are entitled.

The policy of such a measure is plain from the fact that the civil rights of millions of the native population of the United States are destroyed in certain parts of the country on the ground of color; that this invasion springs from the spirit and habit of slavery, and that, if not corrected by the supreme authority, the inevitable result will be a confirmation of that spirit, and a consequent perpetual menace of the public peace ... Nothing can tend so surely to confirm the peace of the Union as the kindly but firmly expressed intention of the Government to protect and enforce the equal civil rights of every citizen.

—From "The Civil Rights Bill," *Harper's Weekly* (April 14, 1866).

CONSIDER THIS

1. Why does the writer believe that it is necessary to define the "true meaning of citizenship"?
2. What does he believe would be the result of not defining citizenship?

KEY TERMS AND CONCEPTS

From "The Civil Rights Bill" editorial:
menace A harmful person or thing.
redress To right a wrong.

From the Fourteenth Amendment to the Constitution:
abridge To limit or shorten.
apportioned Divided and distributed.
due process of the law Fair treatment by the legal system.
immunity Protection.
naturalized Given citizenship.

The Fourteenth Amendment to the US Constitution

Republicans were afraid that the Civil Rights Act did not go far enough to protect the rights and security of African Americans. Even before the bill was passed, the Joint Committee on Reconstruction began working on a constitutional amendment. It would prevent former Confederates from returning to power and guarantee basic civil rights to all citizens, black and white. The amendment also was meant to encourage Southern states to grant black suffrage. It would reduce the congressional representation of states that did not give black men the vote. This reduction would mean that a state would have less representation in Congress, which would mean fewer opportunities to influence federal laws. Congress passed the Fourteenth Amendment on June 13, 1866. It was not ratified by the required number of states until 1868. Following are the first three sections of the amendment.

> Section 1. All persons born or naturalized in the United States, and subject to the jurisdiction thereof, are citizens of the United States and of the state wherein they reside. No state shall make or enforce any law which shall abridge the privileges or immunities of citizens of the United States; nor shall any state deprive any person of life, liberty, or property, without due process of law; nor deny to any person within its jurisdiction the equal protection of the laws.
>
> Section 2. Representatives shall be apportioned among the several states according to their respective numbers, counting the whole number of persons in each state, excluding Indians not taxed. But when the right to vote at any election ... is denied to any of the male inhabitants of such state [who are] citizens of the United States, ... the basis of representation therein shall be reduced ...
>
> Section 3. No person shall be a Senator or Representative in Congress ... or hold any office, civil or military, under the United States, or under any state, who ... shall have engaged in insurrection or rebellion against the same.
>
> —From the Fourteenth Amendment to the US Constitution (1868). Available online at http://www.law.cornell.edu/constitution/constitution.amendmentxiv.html.

CONSIDER THIS

1. What actions does the amendment prohibit states from taking?
2. The writers of the amendment hoped that future lawmakers would be able to broaden its protections. Which phrases in Section 1 do you think were left deliberately unclear in order to allow for later interpretations?

The Military Moves In

Ten of the Southern state governments established under President Johnson's Reconstruction plan refused to ratify the Fourteenth Amendment. The only exception was Tennessee. It approved the amendment and was readmitted to the Union in July 1866.

In response, Congress passed a bill abolishing the existing Southern governments and placing the South under military rule in 1867. The legislation was called the First Reconstruction Act. It required the seceded states to adopt new constitutions ratifying the Fourteenth Amendment and granting voting rights to black men. On March 2, 1867, President Johnson vetoed the bill. On that same day, Congress passed it over his veto.

Three additional Reconstruction Acts were passed: two in 1867 and one in 1868. These laws spelled out the complete details of Congressional Reconstruction. They outlined how new constitutions should be constructed and passed in the Southern states before they could be readmitted to the Union. Here are portions of the First Reconstruction Act.

> Be it enacted, That [the] rebel States shall be divided into military districts and made subject to the military authority of the United States …

Section 2. That it shall be the duty of the President to assign to the command of each of said districts an officer of the army ... and to detail a sufficient military force to enable such officer to perform his duties and enforce his authority ...

Section 3. That it shall be the duty of each officer assigned as aforesaid, to protect all persons in their rights of person and property, to suppress insurrection, disorder, and violence, and to punish, or cause to be punished, all disturbers of the public peace ...

Section 5. That when the people of any one of said rebel States shall have formed a constitution of government in conformity with the Constitution of the United States in all respects, framed by a convention of delegates elected by the male citizens of said State, twenty-one years old and upward, of whatever race, color, or previous condition, ... except such as may be dis[en]franchised for participation in the rebellion or for felony at common law, and when such constitution shall provide that the elective franchise shall be enjoyed by all ... persons ... , and when said State ... shall have adopted the [Fourteenth] amendment to the Constitution of the United States, ... said State shall be declared entitled to representation in Congress ...

Section 6. That, until the people of said rebel States shall be by law admitted to representation in the Congress of the United States, any civil governments which may exist therein shall be deemed provisional only, and in all respects subject to the paramount authority of the United States.

KEY TERMS AND CONCEPTS

From the First Reconstruction Act:
paramount Supreme.
provisional Temporary.
suppress To put an end to.

From President Johnson's message to Congress:
arduous Difficult.
avowedly Stated publicly.
confer upon To give to.
manifestly Clearly.
unpropitious Unfavorable.

—From George P. Sanger, ed., *The Statutes at Large: Treaties and Proclamations of the United States of America from December 1865 to March 1867,* Volume 14 (Boston: Little, Brown, and Company, 1868).

CONSIDER THIS

1. What were the responsibilities of the military governors of the five Southern districts?
2. How could Southern states regain their representation in Congress?

President Johnson Opposes the Reconstruction Acts

In a December 1867 message to Congress, President Johnson explained his opposition to the Reconstruction Acts. He called for Congress to repeal, or to get rid of, them. One of his main arguments was that the acts would establish governments dominated by the freedmen. He believed African Americans were incapable of carrying out the rights and responsibilities of leadership.

> It is manifestly and avowedly the object of these laws to confer upon negroes the privilege of voting and to dis[en]franchise such a number of white citizens as will give ... [black voters] a clear majority at all elections in the Southern States ...
>
> It is not proposed merely that they shall govern themselves, but that they shall rule the white race, make and administer State laws, elect Presidents and members of Congress, and shape ... the future destiny of the whole country. Would such a trust and power be safe in such hands? ...
>
> The plan of putting the Southern States wholly and the General Government partially into the hands of negroes is proposed at a time peculiarly unpropitious. The foundations of society have been broken up by civil war. Industry must be reorganized, justice reestablished, ... and order brought out of confusion. To accomplish these ends would require all the wisdom and virtue of the great men who formed our institutions originally. I confidently believe that their descendants will be equal to the arduous task

before them, but it is worse than madness to expect that negroes will perform it for us.

—From President Johnson's "Third Annual Message to Congress, December 3, 1867." In James D. Richardson, ed., A *Compilation of the Messages and Papers of the Presidents*, Volume VI (Washington, DC: US Government Printing Office, 1897).

CONSIDER THIS

1. How would you respond to President Johnson's argument that it was dangerous to give inexperienced black voters a lot of power?

The House of Representatives Moves to Impeach Johnson

President Johnson could not prevent Congress from passing the Reconstruction Acts. However, he could use the power of his office to weaken their impact. One of the ways the president defied Congress was by firing government officials who were serious about enforcing the laws. His actions outraged Radical Republicans and turned many former supporters against him.

In early 1868, the power struggle reached its peak when Johnson fired Secretary of War Edwin Stanton. The secretary was a supporter of Congressional Reconstruction. After Johnson dismissed Stanton, the House of Representatives voted to impeach the him.

In the impeachment process, the House of Representatives charges a president with "high crimes and misdemeanors." In other words, impeachment takes place when the House believes the president has acted criminally. After the House brings about the charges, the Senate must determine whether he is guilty. If the president is found guilty, he is then removed from office.

The House of Representatives drafted the charges against Andrew Johnson in hopes of impeaching him.

The first eight of the eleven charges against Johnson dealt with his violation of the Tenure of Office Act. The act prohibited the president from dismissing federal officials without Senate approval. He fired Edwin Stanton without approval, so he was, indeed, in violation of the act.

> Article I. That said Andrew Johnson, President of the United States, ... unmindful of the high duties of his office, of his oath of office, and of the requirement of the Constitution that he should take care that the laws be faithfully executed, did unlawfully and in violation of the Constitution and laws of the United States issue an order in writing for the removal of Edwin M. Stanton from the office of Secretary for the Department of War ...with intent then and there to violate the act entitled "An act regulating the tenure of certain civil offices" ...
>
> Article X. That said Andrew Johnson, President of the United States, unmindful of the high duties of his office and the dignity and proprieties thereof, and of the harmony and courtesies which ought to exist and be maintained between the executive and legislative branches of the Government of the United States, ... did attempt to bring into disgrace, ridicule, hatred, contempt, and reproach the Congress of the United States ... and to excite the odium and resentment of all the good people of the United States against Congress and the laws [that] it duly and constitutionally enacted [and did] make and deliver with a loud voice certain intemperate, inflammatory, and scandalous harangues, and did therein utter loud threats and bitter menaces, as well against Congress as the laws of the United States.

—From "Proceedings of the Senate Sitting for the Trial of Andrew Johnson, President of the United States, in Articles of Impeachment exhibited by the House of Representatives." In Henry Steele Commager, ed., *Documents of American History*, 6th edition. (New York: Appleton-Century-Crofts, 1958).

CONSIDER THIS

1. Which article makes it clear that the real reason for Johnson's impeachment was his opposition to Congress?
2. What words and phrases reflect the strong emotions behind the Republicans' attempt to remove Johnson from office?

Senator Sumner Calls for Johnson's Removal

Andrew Johnson's impeachment trial began on March 4, 1868. A number of senators argued for convicting the president. Some senators spoke out in Johnson's defense. Even some Republicans who personally opposed Johnson's Democratic policies were worried. They thought that removing him from office would weaken the executive branch of government. They were also worried that removing him would encourage future lawmakers to impeach any president who disagreed with them.

While some senators were concerned, others were vocal about their support of impeachment. These senators included Radical Republican leader Charles Sumner from Massachusetts, whose speech is excerpted below.

On May 16, the Senate voted on the final article of impeachment. The final article charged the president's dismissal of Stanton as "a high misdemeanor in office." Thirty-five senators found Johnson guilty. As mentioned before, this meant that the

KEY TERMS AND CONCEPTS

From the charges against President Johnson:
harangue An aggressive speech.
intemperate Unrestrained.
odium Widespread disgust for a person or their actions.
proprieties Responsibilities or expectations of behavior.
reproach Disapproval.

From Senator Charles Sumner's speech:
assailing Violently attacking or strongly criticizing.
vindication The act of clearing one's name from blame.

Senate was just one vote short of the two-thirds necessary to convict him. After a second vote taken ten days later generated the same result, the president was cleared of all charges.

> This is one of the last great battles with slavery. Driven from these legislative chambers, driven from the field of war, this monstrous power has found a refuge in the Executive Mansion, where, in utter disregard of the Constitution and laws, it seeks to exercise its ancient, far-reaching sway...
>
> Slavery has been our worst enemy, assailing all, murdering our children, filling our homes with

Like Thaddeus Stevens, Charles Sumner was a leading Radical Republican. As a senator, he was vocal about wanting to remove Johnson from office.

> mourning, and darkening the land with tragedy; and now it rears its crest anew, with Andrew Johnson as its representative ...
>
> He took to himself legislative powers in the reconstruction of the Rebel states; and, ... in vindication of this misconduct, uttered a scandalous speech in which he openly charged members of Congress with being assassins, and mentioned some by name ...

More than one person was appointed provisional governor who could not take the oath of office required by act of Congress ... The effect of these appointments was disastrous. They were in the nature of notice to Rebels everywhere, that participation in the rebellion was no bar to office ... And thus all offices from governor to constable were handed over to a disloyal scramble ...

The powers of the Senate over appointments were trifled with and disregarded by reappointing persons who had been already rejected ... The veto power conferred by the Constitution as a remedy for ill-considered legislation was turned by him into a weapon of offense against Congress ... The power of removal, which Patriot presidents had exercised so sparingly, was seized as an engine of tyranny and openly employed to maintain his wicked purposes ...

Laws enacted by Congress for the benefit of the colored race ... were first attacked by his veto; and when finally passed by the requisite majority over his veto, were treated by him as little better than dead letters ...

For all these, or any one of them, Andrew Johnson should have been impeached and expelled from office.

—From "Charles Sumner, Opinion on the Trial of Andrew Johnson, 1868." Reprinted in Brenda Stalcup, ed., *Reconstruction* (San Diego, CA: Greenhaven Press, 1995).

CONSIDER THIS

1. Are Sumner's arguments based more on facts or emotions? What words and phrases back up your answer?
2. Do you find his arguments convincing? Why or why not?

The Rise of the Radicals

Although Andrew Johnson was cleared of the charges brought against him in his impeachment trial, the controversy had left him with little remaining power or influence. Congress was able to pass acts and amendments that served Republican interests and gave freedmen more rights. Additionally, Johnson's term was coming to an end, and the Republicans had another leader in mind.

General Ulysses S. Grant was the commander in chief, or the head, of the Union armies from 1864 until the end of the Civil War. The popular hero easily won the election and served as president from 1869 until 1877. During his two terms in office, Radicals dominated the Republican Party and shaped Reconstruction policy.

This political cartoon depicts Southerners' opinions of Northerners who moved to the South to help with Reconstruction. They often called them carpetbaggers.

5 Radical Rule

By the end of 1870, all of the Southern states had been readmitted to the Union under the terms of the Reconstruction Acts. The new state governments were dominated by the pro-Reconstruction Republican Party. These governments were largely made up of three groups: black Southerners, white Northerners, and white Southerners who supported Reconstruction.

The Benefits of Reconstruction

The mission of the Reconstruction governments was to restore the Southern economy and protect the freedmen's rights. Southern legislatures directed the rebuilding of roads, bridges, and public buildings. They also devoted funds for the construction of new railroads and established statewide public school systems. These schools offered millions of children, black and white, an opportunity for a free education for the first time. Additionally, the

Reconstruction governments passed laws designed to ensure that African Americans could participate as full citizens in Southern economic and political life. For instance, with the passage of the Fifteenth Amendment, black men could vote for the first time.

White Southerners' Frustrations

Despite these accomplishments, the majority of white Southerners bitterly disliked being governed by Northerners and former slaves. The white Northerners largely moved to the South in search of political office. They were often known as "carpetbaggers," a term generally used to describe a person who seeks political office in a place where they have no connections.

The white Southerners who supported Reconstruction were also seen negatively by their opponents. They were termed "scalawags," a term generally used to describe someone who behaves badly. In both cases, the angry white Southerners saw these individuals who supported Reconstruction as their enemies. White Southerners often believed that carpetbaggers and scalawags supported Reconstruction mostly because they were seeking personal profit.

Claiming that the new governments were useless and corrupt, these opponents worked to restore white rule and overthrow the Reconstruction governments. Opponents of Reconstruction were right about one thing: government corruption did become increasingly widespread in the years following the Civil War. However, politicians who used their political power for personal gain could be found just about everywhere—in the North and South, Republican and Democratic Parties, federal and local governments.

Henry McNeal Turner Takes a Stand

On average, about 15 to 20 percent of the officeholders in Reconstruction governments were black men. To supporters of Reconstruction, black men governing states that had recently held them in bondage was an inspiring sign of social progress. To opponents, it was an outrage.

In 1868, Democrats in the Georgia legislature attempted to get rid of black officials. The white Democrats claimed that the black men were unfit to serve. Among the black representatives was Henry McNeal Turner. Turner had been born to free black parents in Columbia, South Carolina. After the war, he moved to Georgia. There, he helped organize the state's Republican Party and won election to the Georgia House of Representatives.

In the following speech to the Georgia legislature, he defended the right of black people to hold political office. He warned of the consequences if that right was denied. Despite his moving speech, Georgia Democrats succeeded in dismissing fifteen black congressmen. Two years later, however, the federal government forced Georgia to readmit its black legislators.

> I hold that I am a member of this body … I shall neither fawn nor cringe before any party, nor stoop to beg them for my rights … I am here to demand my rights, and to hurl thunderbolts at the men who would dare to cross the threshold of my manhood …
>
> [Black men] have pioneered civilization here; we have built up your country; we have worked in your fields, and garnered your harvests, for two hundred and fifty years! And what do we ask of you in return? … We ask you, now, for our rights …

You may expel us, gentlemen, but I firmly believe that you will someday repent it. The black man cannot protect a country, if the country doesn't protect him; and if, tomorrow, a war should arise, I would not raise a musket to defend a country where my manhood is denied ... Where have you ever heard of four millions of freemen being governed by laws, and yet have no hand in their making? ... How dare you to make laws by which to try me and my wife and children, and deny me a voice in the making of these laws? ...

You may think you are doing yourselves honor by expelling us from this House; but when we go, we will ... light a torch of truth that will never be extinguished ... When you expel us, you make us forever your political foes, and you will never find a black man to vote a Democratic ticket again.

—From Henry McNeal Turner's speech to the Georgia Legislature, September 3, 1868. In Edwin S. Redkey, ed., *Respect Black: The Writings and Speeches of Henry McNeal Turner* (New York: Arno Press, 1971).

CONSIDER THIS

1. How does Turner justify his demand for the right of black men to hold political office?
2. What does he say will happen if that right is denied?

KEY TERMS AND CONCEPTS

From Henry McNeal Turner's speech:

fawn To give someone exaggerated praise or flattery, in order to gain favor.

foe An enemy.

repent To express regret over a wrongdoing.

From Louis Freeland Post's account:

consequent Resulting.

"Empire" to our "Palmetto" State New York to South Carolina.

graft The acquiring of money by illegal or unfair means.

Louis Freeland Post: A "Carpetbagger"

In addition to black politicians, there were white politicians from the North that white Southerners disliked. A number of Northerners moved south after the Civil War to take part in the region's political reorganization. These Northern white officeholders became a significant force in Southern state governments.

Frustrated white Southerners gave the unwelcome visitors a negative nickname: carpetbagger. The term came from the name for a common type of traveler's bag made of carpet material. According to Southern critics, the carpetbaggers were crooks who came to rob the state treasuries, or government funds. The critics suggested that these Northerners carried all their worldly possessions in a carpetbag. In reality, most of the so-called carpetbaggers were

Freedmen's Bureau officials. They were former Union soldiers, teachers, clergymen, or businessmen.

In the following account, Northerner Louis Freeland Post describes how he became known as a carpetbagger in South Carolina.

> Ten years after the secession of South Carolina and less than six after the close of the consequent Civil War between the States, I became a South Carolina "carpetbagger." That is, I migrated from our "Empire" to our "Palmetto" State. Five years before, I had migrated from New Jersey, my native state, to New York; twenty-five years after that from New York to Ohio, and two years later from Ohio to Illinois—all without being called a "carpetbagger." But I was called a "carpetbagger" in South Carolina when in 1870 I migrated to that State from New York ...
>
> All immigrants to South Carolina from our Northern States in the late 1860's and the early 1870's were called "carpetbaggers," if while there they got a living—more or less of it, and whether by honest earnings or dishonest graft—in connection with the public service. Those also who got their living in private employment, but who associated with the office-holding class, were called "carpetbaggers"; and those who pursued unofficial callings and had few official associates or none became "carpetbaggers" upon going into politics. This if they were from any of our Northern States. If natives of South Carolina, they became "scalawags," regardless of any previous condition of honor or respectability.

—From Louis F. Post, "A 'Carpetbagger' in South Carolina," *Journal of Negro History*, No. 1 (1925). Reprinted in James P. Shenton, ed., *The Reconstruction: A Documentary History, 1865–1877* (New York: G. P. Putnam's Sons, 1963).

CONSIDER THIS

1. According to the writer, what types of people were called carpetbaggers and scalawags?
2. How do you think the writer felt about being called a carpetbagger?

Booker T. Washington was passionate about education. He was influential in conversations about African Americans and their rights after the end of the Reconstruction Era.

Booker T. Washington's *Up from Slavery*

Despite name-calling, the Radical Republicans were able to push through some strong programs in the South. For instance, before the Civil War, few Southerners, white or black, had access to a free education. During Reconstruction, state governments established public school systems throughout the South, replacing and expanding the network of freedmen's schools. Charitable organizations also founded colleges and trade schools to offer black men and women the chance for higher learning. One person to benefit from these opportunities was Booker T. Washington.

Born into slavery in 1856 and freed at age seven by the Emancipation Proclamation, Washington attended one of the South's first public schools for black children. He completed his education at the Hampton Normal and Agricultural Institute (now Hampton University) in Virginia. He went on to become a famous public speaker, educator, and the founder of Tuskegee Institute in Alabama. In his autobiography, *Up from Slavery*, Washington describes the challenges and excitement of getting an education.

> One day, while at work in the coal-mine, I happened to overhear two miners talking about a great school for coloured people somewhere in Virginia. This was the first time I had ever heard anything about any kind of school or college that was more pretentious than the little coloured school in our town …
>
> As they went on describing the school, it seemed to me that it must be the greatest place on earth, and not even Heaven presented more attractions for me at that time than did the Hampton Normal and Agricultural Institute in Virginia, about which these men were talking. I resolved at once to go to that

school, although I had no idea where it was, or how many miles away, or how I was going to reach it ...

I reached Hampton, with a surplus of exactly fifty cents with which to begin my education. To me it had been a long, eventful journey; but the first sight of the large, three-story, brick school building seemed to have rewarded me for all that I had undergone in order to reach the place ... It seemed to me to be the largest and most beautiful building I had ever seen. The sight of it seemed to give me new life. I felt that a new kind of existence had now begun—that life would now have a new meaning. I felt that I had reached the promised land, and I resolved to let no obstacle prevent me from putting forth the highest effort to fit myself to accomplish the most good in the world ...

I was among the youngest of the students who were in Hampton at that time. Most of the students were men and women—some as old as forty years of age. As I now recall the scene of my first year, I do not believe that one often has the opportunity of coming into contact with three or four hundred men and women who were so tremendously in earnest as these men and women were. Every hour was occupied in study or work. Nearly all had had enough actual contact with the world to teach them the need of education. Many of the older ones were, of course, too old to master the text-books very thoroughly, and it was often sad to watch their struggles; but they made up in earnestness much of what they lacked in books. Many of them were as poor as I was, and,

KEY TERMS AND CONCEPTS

From Booker T. Washington's *Up from Slavery*:

fifty cents Approximately one day's salary for most unskilled laborers in the mid-nineteenth century.

pretentious Ambitious.

surplus A leftover amount.

besides having to wrestle with their books, they had to struggle with a poverty which prevented their having the necessities of life.

—From Booker T. Washington, *Up from Slavery: An Autobiography* (New York: Doubleday, 1963).

CONSIDER THIS

1. What did the opportunity to go to college mean to Washington?
2. What challenges did the freed slaves face in getting an education?

The Fifteenth Amendment to the US Constitution

In addition to setting up educational facilities, the Radical Republicans were able to pass major legislation like the Reconstruction Acts and the Fourteenth Amendment. Most of the legislation passed was focused on fixing problems in the South.

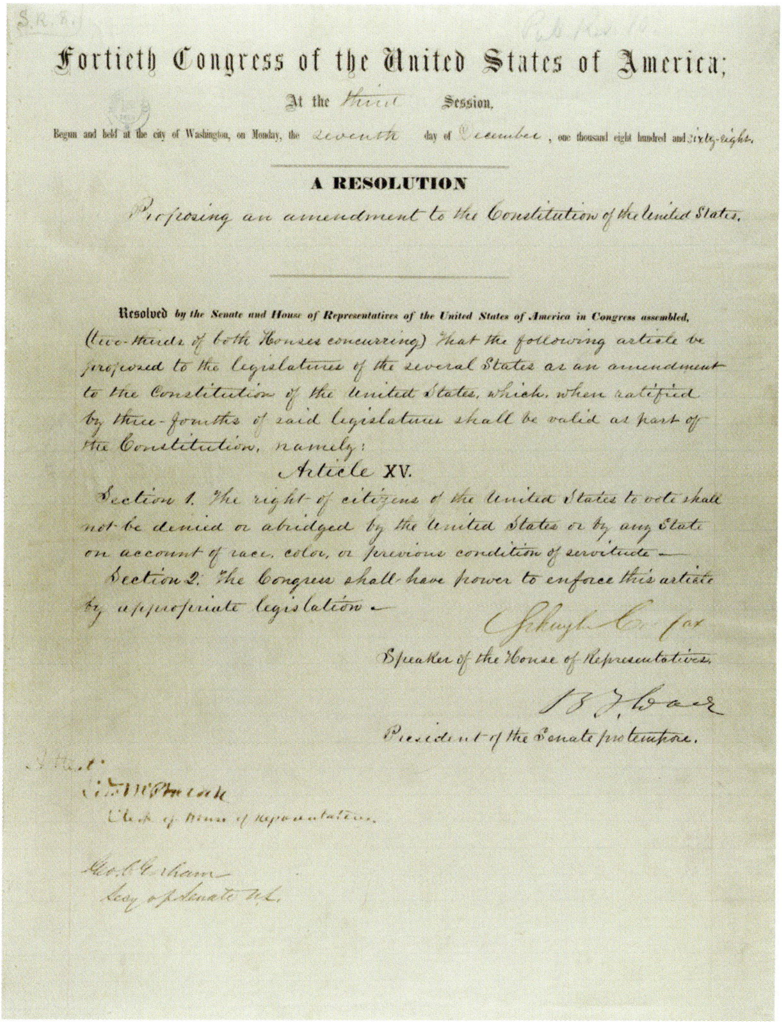

Fortieth Congress of the United States of America;

At the third Session,

Begun and held at the city of Washington, on Monday, the seventh day of December, one thousand eight hundred and sixty-eight.

A RESOLUTION

Proposing an amendment to the Constitution of the United States.

Resolved by the Senate and House of Representatives of the United States of America in Congress assembled, (two-thirds of both Houses concurring) That the following article be proposed to the legislatures of the several States as an amendment to the Constitution of the United States, which, when ratified by three-fourths of said legislatures shall be valid as part of the Constitution, namely:

Article XV.

Section 1. The right of citizens of the United States to vote shall not be denied or abridged by the United States or by any State on account of race, color, or previous condition of servitude—

Section 2. The Congress shall have power to enforce this article by appropriate legislation—

Schuyler Colfax
Speaker of the House of Representatives.

B. F. Wade
President of the Senate pro tempore.

Attest
Edw McPherson
Clerk of House of Representatives.

Geo. C. Gorham
Secy of Senate U.S.

The Fifteenth Amendment gave African American men the right to vote.

However, in February 1869, Congress set out to resolve an injustice that affected the entire nation.

While the Reconstruction Acts required Southern states to grant black suffrage, black men still could not vote in most Northern states. In 1869, Congress addressed that problem by proposing the Fifteenth Amendment. The amendment forbids any state from denying any male citizens the right to vote on the grounds of "race, color, or previous condition of servitude." All Southern states that had not yet been reconstructed were required to approve the amendment before they could rejoin the Union. The amendment was ratified in February 1870.

> Section 1. The right of citizens of the United States to vote shall not be denied or abridged by the United States or by any state on account of race, color, or previous condition of servitude.
>
> Section 2. The Congress shall have power to enforce this article by appropriate legislation.
>
> —From the Fifteenth Amendment to the US Constitution. Available online at http://www.law.cornell.edu/constitution/constitution.amendmentxv.html.

CONSIDER THIS

1. Radical Republicans proposed a form of the Fifteenth Amendment that forbade states from imposing additional conditions for voting, such as literacy tests or property ownership requirements. Do you think those extra protections should have been added?
2. Why do you think moderates might have opposed the stronger version of the amendment?

The Civil Rights Act of 1875

Slavery was dead. Citizenship and suffrage were secured by the end of 1870. However, racial prejudice and discrimination were still very much alive in the United States. For these reasons, Senator Charles Sumner introduced a second Civil Rights Bill in 1870. He proposed it to combat what he called "the last lingering taint [stain] of slavery." Sumner's bill prohibited discrimination in schools, juries, public transportation, and public facilities such as restaurants and theaters.

White Southerners argued that the proposed legislation was unconstitutional because it was aimed at controlling private businesses and individuals. Many lawmakers also feared that the measure would destroy the South's new system of public schools, which were segregated. These lawmakers were concerned that white people would refuse to allow their children to attend school alongside black children.

Despite these doubts, Congress finally approved the bill in February 1875, five years after it had initially been proposed and a year after Senator Sumner's death in 1874. In its final version, the Civil Rights Act of 1875 did not address segregation in schools.

> Be it enacted, That all persons within the jurisdiction of the United States shall be entitled to the full and equal enjoyment of the accommodations, advantages, facilities, and privileges of inns, public conveyances on land or water, theaters, and other places of public amusement; subject only to the conditions and limitations established by law, and applicable alike to citizens of every race and color, regardless of any previous condition of servitude.
>
> Section 2. That any person who shall violate the foregoing section by denying to any citizen ... the

> enjoyment of any of the accommodations, advantages, facilities, or privileges ... shall, for every such offense, forfeit and pay the sum of five hundred dollars to the person aggrieved thereby ...
>
> Section 4. That no citizen possessing all other qualifications which are or may be prescribed by law shall be disqualified for service as juror in any court of the United States, or of any State, on account of race, color, or previous condition of servitude.
>
> —From the Civil Rights Act of 1875.

CONSIDER THIS

1. What protections does the act extend to black citizens?
2. How would you answer arguments that Congress should not pass laws regulating private businesses and individuals?

John R. Lynch Denounces Segregation

Even though Congress had good intentions, the Civil Rights Act of 1875 had little effect on racial discrimination. Most public facilities in the South continued to discriminate against black people. These places would either deny black people service or confine them to separate, segregated areas.

In the following address to Congress, Representative John R. Lynch describes the segregation he encountered on his official trips to Washington, DC. Born into slavery, Lynch had been elected as US representative from Mississippi in 1873.

Republican John Lynch served in the Mississippi House of Representatives and in the US Congress.

Think of it for a moment; here am I, a member of your honorable body, representing one of the largest and wealthiest districts in the State of Mississippi, and possibly in the South; a district composed of persons of different races, religions, and nationalities; and yet, when I leave my home to come to the capital of the nation to take part in the deliberations of the House and to participate with you in making laws for the government of this great Republic, ... I am treated, not as an American citizen, but as a brute. Forced to occupy a filthy smoking-car both night and day, with drunkards, gamblers, and criminals; and for what? Not that I am unable or unwilling to pay my way; not that I am obnoxious in my personal appearance or disrespectful in my conduct; but simply because I happen to be of a darker complexion. If this treatment was confined to persons of our own sex we could possibly afford to endure it. But such is not the case. Our wives and our daughters, our sisters and our mothers, are subjected to the same insults and to the same uncivilized treatment ... The only moments of my life when I am necessarily compelled to question my loyalty to my Government or my devotion to the flag of my country is when I read of outrages having been committed upon innocent colored people ... and when I leave my home to go traveling.

Mr. Speaker, if this unjust discrimination is to be longer tolerated by the American people, which I do not, cannot, and will not believe until I am forced to do so, then I can only say with sorrow and regret that our boasted civilization is a fraud; our republican institutions a failure; our social system a disgrace; and our religion a complete hypocrisy.

—From John R. Lynch, speech to Congress, February 3, 1875. Reprinted in William L. Katz, *Eyewitness: The Negro in American History* (New York: Pitman Publishing, 1968).

CONSIDER THIS

1. How was Lynch discriminated against on his trips to Washington?
2. Are his arguments against discrimination based on facts, emotions, or a combination of both?

The End on the Horizon

For every step forward that the Radical Republicans made in Congress, racial prejudice and the frustrations of Southerners reared their ugly heads. Most white Southerners bitterly opposed Reconstruction. They were still angry and humiliated over the loss of the Civil War. They resented the continued presence of Northern troops and Freedmen's Bureau officials in the South. They also objected to the high taxes they were forced to pay to fund all the Reconstruction programs. Their hostility toward Reconstruction would soon halt the Radical Republican success.

The Ku Klux Klan, a white supremacist group, is a terrorist group that was founded after the Civil War.

6

From Reconstruction to Regression

Over time, Reconstruction opponents united in their efforts to overthrow the new Southern state governments. Calling for an end to Northern "oppression," they pressured the scalawags to return to the "white man's party." In states with a large white population, that was often enough to vote the Republicans out of office. Elsewhere, terrorist groups such as the Ku Klux Klan used intimidation and violence to force freedmen and white Republicans to vote for the Democrats or not vote at all.

The Rise of White Supremacy

The Ku Klux Klan was a group of white supremacists. Established in the aftermath of the Civil War by former members of the Confederate army, the Klan was just one of the groups active in resisting Radical Reconstruction. Another, called the Knights of the White Camelia, had a similar purpose and mission. Often, these terrorist groups beat and killed freedmen and the white people who supported Radical Reconstruction.

Between 1868 and 1870, the Klan wreaked havoc on the South. Congress responded by passing laws to limit the power and reach of the Ku Klux Klan and others who wanted to infringe upon the rights of freedmen. The Enforcement Act of 1870 was the first of three acts that Congress passed to protect voting rights of black men. It banned the sort of terrorist strategies the Klan used to intimidate black voters. The Second and Third Enforcement Acts, both passed in 1871, worked in similar ways. They allowed federal officials to oversee local and state elections. These acts also made some of the intimidation strategies that the Klan used illegal, and they allowed the president to use the military to prevent such behavior. The Third Enforcement Act is also called the Ku Klux Klan Act.

White Southerners Regain Power

In spite of the acts and amendments Congress passed, white Southerners regained power in the South. By the late 1870s, Democrats had regained control of all Southern state governments. Additionally, the federal government saw a change in the executive branch.

Although President Ulysses S. Grant was interested in protecting the rights of black people through the Fifteenth Amendment and the Enforcement Acts, he was not terribly effective. Southerners continued to be frustrated with Reconstruction. Similarly, Northerners were exhausted with failed attempts to fix the South's issues. People were ready for a change as Grant's second term came to an end in 1877.

The 1876 presidential election was an opportunity for that change. Republican Rutherford B. Hayes ran against Democrat

Samuel J. Tilden. It was projected that Tilden would win; however, there was an election dispute. During the dispute, Hayes was able to get the final votes he needed by promising that the would allow Democratic rule in the South if elected. Ultimately, Hayes won the election.

After Hayes was inaugurated in 1877, he followed through with his promise. He promptly withdrew federal troops that were stationed in the South. These troops were there to do things like make sure that black men could vote without interference. The removal of these troops promised a return of unchecked white supremacy and Democratic Party rule in the South.

Hayes's decision effectively ended the Reconstruction Era. In the years that followed, Southern legislatures would pass laws depriving African Americans of their civil rights and enforcing a rigid segregation of the races. The consequences of Hayes's decision would be long lasting.

A Song for the Rebels

The song "O I'm a Good Old Rebel" was popular in the South long after the end of the Civil War. It is believed that the lyrics were written by Innes Randolph, a former Confederate officer. They expressed commonly held attitudes toward emancipation and the Reconstruction process.

> O, I'm a good old Rebel,
> Now that's just what I am,
> For this "Fair Land of Freedom"
> I do not give a damn!
> I'm glad I fit against it,
> I only wish we'd won,
> And I don't want no pardon
> For anything I've done.

KEY TERMS AND CONCEPTS

From "O I'm a Good Old Rebel":

fit Fought.

wuss and wuss Worse and worse.

From Ku Klux Klan oath:

bequeath To leave to someone.

divulge To make known.

immaculate Free from sin or error.

pecuniary Relating to money.

I hates the Constitution,
This "Great Republic," too!
I hates the Freedman's Bureau
In uniforms of blue!
I hates the nasty eagle,
With all his brags and fuss,
And the lying, thieving Yankees,
I hates 'em wuss and wuss.

—"O I'm a Good Old Rebel" (1861). Retrieved from the Library of Congress, https://www.loc.gov/item/ihas.200002507.

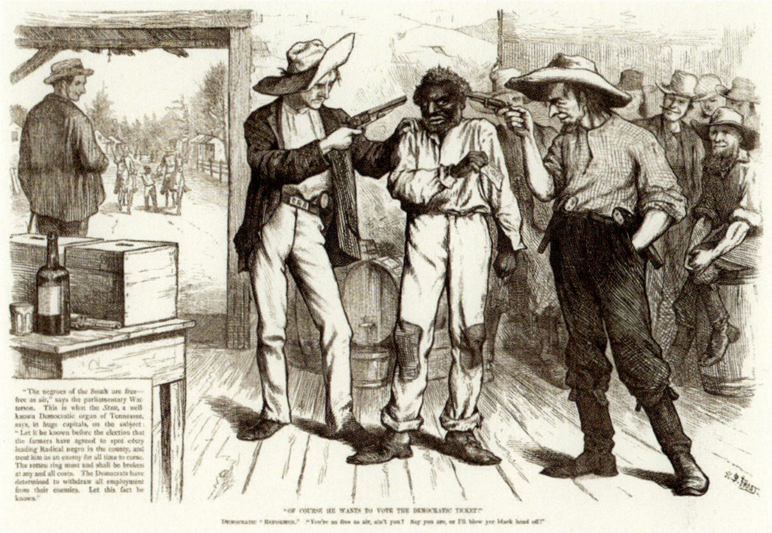

This 1876 political cartoon demonstrates how white Southern Democrats might have used scare tactics to influence black people's votes.

CONSIDER THIS

1. Many Southerners continued to fight the Civil War long after it was over, in some cases for decades. Was there any advantage to this kind of thinking, or would they have benefited from letting their anger go?
2. What effects do these decades of fighting have on our society today?

The Klan's Oath

In the late 1860s, resistance to Radical Reconstruction became increasingly violent. White supremacists formed secret societies to combat the political power of the freedmen and their supporters.

The largest and most brutal of these organizations was the "Invisible Empire of the South," commonly known as the Ku Klux Klan.

Organized around 1866 by Confederate veterans in Tennessee, the group used intimidation and violence to keep African Americans and white Republicans from voting. Klan members wore ghostly white robes and hoods to disguise their identities and frighten the superstitious. They burned homes, schoolhouses, and churches. They whipped, tortured, or lynched thousands of people. A lynching is a public murder, often by hanging, usually by a group of people.

In 1871, President Grant appointed a federal grand jury to investigate Ku Klux Klan activities. The jury's report included this copy of the loyalty oath taken by new Klan members. The report recommended that the president use "the strong arm of the government" to suppress, or to put an end to, the Klan and similar terrorist groups.

> I, __________, before the immaculate Judge of Heaven and earth, and upon the Holy Evangelists of Almighty God, do, of my own free will and accord, subscribe to the following sacredly binding obligation:
>
> 1. We are on the side of justice, humanity, and constitutional liberty, as bequeathed to us in its purity by our forefathers.
>
> 2. We oppose and reject the principles of the Radical Party.
>
> 3. We pledge mutual aid to each other in sickness, distress, and pecuniary embarrassment.

4. Female friends, widows, and their households shall ever be special objects of our regard and protection.

5. Any member divulging, or causing to be divulged, any of the foregoing obligations, shall meet the fearful penalty and traitor's doom, which is Death! Death! Death!

—From "Report of the Federal Grand Jury to the Judges of the U.S. Circuit Court, Columbia, S.C.," 42nd Congress, 2nd session, 1872. Reprinted in Brenda Stalcup, ed., *Reconstruction: Opposing Viewpoints* (San Diego, CA: Greenhaven Press, 1995).

CONSIDER THIS

1. What do you think is meant by the word "purity" in the first section?
2. Why do you think Southern government leaders were hesitant to take action against the Ku Klux Klan?

Mississippi Democrats Steal an Election

When intimidation and violence failed to keep black men and white Republicans from voting, white supremacists often found ways to rig election results. D. J. Foreman was a black Republican leader from a small district in Mississippi. He had overwhelming support from Republican voters. In testimony before a Senate committee investigating voting fraud, he explained how the Democrats had succeeded in "winning" a local election in 1875.

question: What did you propose to do at the election?

answer: Some said not to go to the polls; some said they would go; some said they were afraid to go, and some said they were not, and they would go [even] if they got killed ...

question: Are your people armed generally? ...

answer: No, sir; they are poorly armed ...

question: When did you first know what the result was [in the election]?

answer: I met Bazelius, clerk of the election, the next morning ... , and I asked him what was the result of the election. He told me: "We beat you badly yesterday." I says, "No, you didn't; you polled forty-seven votes." He says, "It was you polled forty-seven votes, and we polled three hundred. You all voted democratic votes." ...

question: Do you know anything more about what took place at the election?

answer: [The whites] met the colored people, and would not allow them to come with arms; and the white people kept on theirs, and that scared the colored people ...

question: And the democrats carried their arms?

answer: Yes, sir; and [they] told me that I would have to shut my mouth.

—From "Mississippi in 1875," Senate Report 527, Part II, 44th Congress, 1st Session. Reprinted in William Loren Katz, *Eyewitness: The Negro in American History* (New York: Pitman Publishing, 1968).

CONSIDER THIS

1. What methods did the Democrats use to steal the election?
2. What steps could the federal government have taken to prevent this case of voting fraud?

The "Compromise" of 1877

By 1876, Democrats had overthrown, or "redeemed," the Reconstruction governments of all but three Southern states: South Carolina, Florida, and Louisiana. That year's presidential election positioned Rutherford B. Hayes, a moderate Republican, against Democratic candidate Samuel J. Tilden.

In the three "unredeemed" states, both sides tried to influence the election's outcome through a variety of illegal means. These illegal measures included bribery, voter intimidation, and miscounting. In the end, each of the states turned in two different sets of returns, or official election reports. One set of returns reported that Hayes won. The other set reported that Tilden had.

To resolve the dispute, Congress appointed a special electoral commission, or a committee with the specific responsibility of overseeing a fair election. It included members from both parties. The commission worked out a compromise that gave the presidency to Hayes. Hayes secured this support by promising to withdraw the federal troops from the South. In his inaugural address, President Hayes expressed the hope that white and black people would work together to peacefully complete the process of Reconstruction.

KEY TERMS AND CONCEPTS

From President Rutherford B. Hayes's inaugural address:
contentment A state of satisfaction.
cordial Friendly.
prosperity The state of success or wealth.

From Frederick Douglass's speech:
calamity A disastrous event.
malignant Evil or infectious.
vulgar Offensive or unrefined.

From the sharecropper's account:
fix us Injure us.
fodder Food or material.
parish A small district or division, often one that is part of a church community.
provisions Supplies, such as food or equipment.
rashings Rations.

The evils which afflict the Southern States can only be removed or remedied by the united and harmonious efforts of both races, actuated by motives of mutual sympathy and regard; and while in duty bound and fully determined to protect the rights of all by every constitutional means at the disposal of my Administration, I am sincerely anxious to use every legitimate influence in favor of honest and efficient local self-government as the true resource of those States for the promotion of the contentment and prosperity of their citizens. In the effort I shall make to accomplish this purpose I ask the cordial cooperation of all who cherish an interest in the welfare of the country, trusting that party ties and the prejudice of race will be freely surrendered in behalf of the great purpose to be accomplished ...

At the basis of all prosperity, for [the South] as well as for every other part of the country, lies the improvement of the intellectual and moral condition of the people. Universal suffrage should rest upon universal education. To this end, liberal and permanent provision should be made for the support of free schools by the State governments, and, if need be, supplemented by legitimate aid from national authority.

Let me assure my countrymen of the Southern States that it is my earnest desire to regard and promote their truest interest—the interests of the white and of the colored people both and equally—and to put forth my best efforts in behalf of a civil policy which will forever wipe out in our political affairs the color line and the distinction between

North and South, to the end that we may have not merely a united North or a united South, but a united country.

—From Rutherford B. Hayes, Inaugural Address, March 5, 1877.

CONSIDER THIS

1. Why does Hayes believe that the races will be able to work together to restore the South?
2. Do you think that his hopes were realistic?

The Civil Rights Act of 1875 Is Unconstitutional

With the overthrow of Republican governments and the withdrawal of federal troops, white rule was restored in the South. New all-white governments rolled back the advances of Reconstruction. They reduced funding for black schools and imposed conditions that made it nearly impossible for African Americans to vote.

Discriminatory laws gradually provided for the strict segregation of the races. In several key decisions, the Supreme Court upheld these laws. The justices ruled that laws designed to protect the rights of African Americans were unconstitutional. In 1883, the court struck down the Civil Rights Act of 1875. In the *Civil Rights Cases* (1883), it ruled that the federal government did not have the right to create laws against discrimination by private businesses and individuals. At a protest meeting in Washington, DC, Frederick Douglass spoke out against the ruling.

This decision has inflicted a heavy calamity upon the seven millions of the colored people of this country, and left them naked and defenceless against the action of a malignant, vulgar and pitiless prejudice.

Sharecroppers, pictured here, leased land on which they worked. They then paid for part of their rent with the crops they harvested.

It presents the United States before the world as a nation utterly destitute of power to protect the rights of its own citizens. It can claim service and allegiance, loyalty and life of them, but it cannot protect them against the most palpable violation of [their] rights …

In the name of common sense, I ask, what right have we to call ourselves a nation in view of this decision and this destitution of power?

In humiliating the colored people of this country, this decision humbles the nation.

—From a speech by Frederick Douglass, October 1883. In Henry McNeal Turner, *The Barbarous Decision of the United States Supreme Court Declaring the Civil Rights Act Unconstitutional*, 1893.

CONSIDER THIS

1. What does Douglass say will be the result of the Supreme Court decision?
2. Why does he believe that the ruling hurts not only African Americans but the entire nation?

Slavery Versus Sharecropping

One of the most significant failures of Reconstruction was in the area of land reform. Radicals had advocated breaking up the old plantations and distributing the land to the freed slaves. However, supporters of this policy were unable to overcome fierce opposition from white Southerners as well as Northern moderates and conservatives.

In the years following the Civil War, many landless freedmen ended up working as sharecroppers on white-owned farms. Sharecroppers earned low wages or a small portion of the harvest from the land they worked in return for their labor. In 1875, a congressional committee investigating working conditions in Louisiana heard the following testimony from three black farmworkers. It illustrates the problems with the sharecropping system.

> We worked, or made contract to work, … on Mr. McMoring's place, and worked for one-third of the crop, and he was to find us all of our provisions; and in July, 1875, we was working alone in the field, and Mr. McMoring and McBounton came to us and says, "Well, boys, you all got to get away from here"; and … the two white men went and got sticks and guns, and told us that we must leave the place; and we told them that we would not leave it, because we don't want to give up our crop for nothing; and they told us that we had better leave, or we would not get anything; and we wanted justice, but [they] would not let us have justice … They beat Isaiah Fuller, and whipped him, and then we got afraid, and we left the place; and we [have] about thirty acres [12 ha] in cotton, and the best cotton crop in that part of the parish; and we have about twenty-nine acres [11.7 ha] of corn, and about the best corn in the parish, and it is ripe, and the fodder ready to pull, and our cotton laid by; and [they] runned us off the place, and told us not to come back any more; and we were due [from] Mr. McMoring the sum of one hundred and eighty dollars and they told us that if they ever heard of it any more that they would fix us; and all the time that we were living and working on

> the place they would not half feed us; and we had to pay for all, or half of our rashings, ... and we worked for them as though we were slaves, and then [were] treated like dogs.
>
> —From Executive Document No. 30, 44th Congress, 2nd Session. Reprinted in Milton Meltzer, *The Black Americans: A History in Their Own Words* (New York: HarperCollins, 1984).

CONSIDER THIS

1. One land reform advocate argued that emancipating the slaves without giving them the land they needed to achieve economic independence was "only the mockery of freedom." How does this document illustrate that point?
2. How were the sharecroppers' working conditions different from their lives under slavery? How were they the same?

The Lasting Effects

After the removal of the troops, the progress that had been made during Reconstruction unraveled. Although historians have long stated that Reconstruction ended in 1877 with this withdrawal of troops, some historians are rethinking this end date.

In the mid-2010s, the National Park Service (NPS) was working on developing a Reconstruction Era National Monument. Eventually, the NPS settled on a group of historical sites in Beaufort County, South Carolina. The county is home to one of the first schools to educate African Americans. Before landing on Beaufort County, however, historians on behalf of the NPS

After the reforms of the Reconstruction Era were reversed, public facilities, from train cars to schools to water fountains, were segregated for decades to come.

went about identifying sites that were "nationally significant" to the era. According to a *New York Times* article about the monument's development, historians have started to believe that the Reconstruction Era lasted until the mid to late 1890s.

This timeline of Reconstruction is supported by decisions made by the judicial branch in the years following the removal of troops from the South. For instance, the Supreme Court ruled that federal protections against discrimination were unconstitutional in the *Civil Rights Cases* (1883). Similarly, the court supported the constitutionality of segregation with its *Plessy v. Ferguson* (1896) decision. The court did not believe that segregation violated African Americans' Fourteenth Amendment right to equal treatment. Its ruling made it legal to segregate public transportation. However, the nationwide practice of segregation would extend far beyond public transportation to many other areas of daily life, including schools, restrooms, and water fountains.

In addition to these Supreme Court rulings, Southern states began to rewrite state constitutions in the 1890s. These new constitutions limited the rights of black people. Similar to Mississippi's earlier black codes, these new state laws imposed restrictions like requiring literacy tests or landownership for men who wanted to vote. Although Reconstruction had provided education to many, there were still plenty of African Americans who could not read. Additionally, with the sharecropping situation, landownership did not come easily for black people.

These problematic laws were only reinforced by the Supreme Court. Just two years after the *Plessy v. Ferguson* decision, the court ruled that Mississippi's measures to disenfranchise black people was constitutional (*Williams v. Mississippi*). Laws that supported segregation and disenfranchisement, known as Jim Crow laws, were thus firmly in place as the country entered the twentieth century.

Despite the work of activists like Booker T. Washington, W. E. B Du Bois, and Ida B. Wells-Barnett in the late nineteenth and early twentieth centuries, segregation and discriminatory laws would last until the mid-twentieth century. The civil rights movement of the 1950s and 1960s, laws like the Civil Rights Act of 1964 and the Voting Rights Act of 1965, and Supreme Court decisions like *Brown v. Board of Education of Topeka* (1954) eventually began to change the tides in the United States.

Unfortunately, however, the failures of the Reconstruction Era would be lasting. Despite some protections by the federal government, discrimination and tensions between white and black Americans continue today.

CHRONOLOGY

1860 Abraham Lincoln is elected president. South Carolina secedes from the Union.

1861 The American Civil War begins at Fort Sumter. Ten more states secede from the Union.

1863 President Lincoln issues the Emancipation Proclamation.

1865 Congress establishes the US Bureau of Refugees, Freedmen, and Abandoned Lands. President Lincoln is assassinated in April, and Andrew Johnson becomes president. The Civil War ends. The Thirteenth Amendment is ratified.

1866 Congress passes the Civil Rights Act of 1866. Congress passes the Fourteenth Amendment. Tennessee becomes the first Southern state to be readmitted to the Union.

1867 Congress passes three Reconstruction Acts.

1868 The House of Representatives votes to impeach President Johnson, but the Senate fails to convict him. The Fourteenth Amendment is ratified. Ulysses S. Grant is elected president. Congress passes an additional Reconstruction Act.

1870 The Fifteenth Amendment is ratified. Congress passes the Enforcement Act. Georgia becomes the last Southern state to be readmitted to the Union.

1871 Congress passes the Second Enforcement Act and the Third Enforcement Act, also known as the Ku Klux Klan Act.

1872 The Freedmen's Bureau expires. Grant is elected to a second term as president.

1875 Congress passes the Civil Rights Act of 1875.

1876 The outcome of the presidential election between Rutherford B. Hayes and Samuel J. Tilden is disputed.

1877 Rutherford B. Hayes is inaugurated as president of the United States. In accordance with the Compromise of 1877, Hayes withdraws the last federal troops from the South, officially ending Reconstruction.

1883 The Supreme Court rules that the Civil Rights Act of 1875 is unconstitutional (*Civil Rights Cases*).

1896 The Supreme Court rules that segregation of public transportation is constitutional (*Plessy v. Ferguson*).

1954 The Supreme Court rules that the segregation of public schools is unconstitutional, which leads to the desegregation of public facilities (*Brown v. Board of Education of Topeka*).

1964 The Civil Rights Act of 1964, which protects people from discrimination based on race, sex, color, religion, or national origin, is passed.

1965 The Voting Rights Act of 1965, aimed at protecting black people's enfranchisement, is passed.

GLOSSARY

denounce To publicly declare as wrong or evil.

disenfranchisement The state of being deprived of a right, especially the right to vote.

Fifteenth Amendment This amendment to the US Constitution guarantees all male citizens the right to vote without regard to that man's "race, color, or previous condition of servitude."

Fourteenth Amendment This amendment to the US Constitution guarantees that all citizens should receive equal protection from the government and equal treatment by the judicial system.

Freedmen's Bureau This agency of the War Department was responsible for protecting former slaves and white Southerners left devastated by the Civil War. It provided food; helped build homes, schools, and public facilities; and helped negotiate labor contracts, among other things.

impeachment The act of charging a public official with crimes, in order to remove the official from office.

legislature A governing body responsible for making laws.

pardon To excuse or forgive someone for wrongdoing.

Radical Republicans A group of Republicans who were responsible for Congressional Reconstruction, which placed harsh restrictions on former Confederates and protected African Americans.

ratify To give formal consent to a legal document, usually by signing.

ration A fixed amount of food given on a regular basis.

Reconstruction Acts The four laws enacted between 1867 and 1868 that outlined the process states had to go through in order to be readmitted to the Union. These provisions included ratifying the Fourteenth Amendment and drafting state constitutions that gave black men the right to vote.

reform To change something in hopes of improving it.

renounce To formally abandon.

secede To formally withdraw from a group or an organization.

segregation The separation of people based on race.

suffrage The right to vote. Also called enfranchisement or elective franchise.

Thirteenth Amendment This amendment to the US Constitution prohibits slavery or involuntary servitude in the United States.

welfare The public health and happiness, or government programs created to ensure public health and happiness.

white supremacy The belief that white people are superior to those of other races.

FURTHER INFORMATION

Books

Baptiste, Tracey. *The Civil War and Reconstruction Eras.* The African American Experience: From Slavery to the Presidency. New York: Britannica Educational Publishing, 2015.

Hamen, Susan E. *Civil War Aftermath and Reconstruction*. Minneapolis: Essential Library, 2017.

Washington, Booker T. *Up from Slavery: An Autobiography* (Townsend Library Edition). West Berlin, NJ: Townsend Press, 2004.

Wright, Barbara. *Crow.* New York: Random House, 2013.

Ziff, Marsha. *The Reconstruction of the South After the Civil War in United States History*. New York: Enslow Publishing, 2014.

Websites

African American Records at the National Archives: Freedmen's Bureau

https://www.archives.gov/research/african-americans/freedmens-bureau

This website provides access to nearly two million records related to the Freedmen's Bureau's work, including records that provide genealogical information.

African American Sites in the Digital Collections: Civil War and Reconstruction
https://www.loc.gov/rr/program/bib/afam/afam-1861.html

This Library of Congress website provides links to online exhibitions and primary-source documents related to the Reconstructions Era.

National Park Service: Reconstruction Era
https://www.nps.gov/reer/index.htm

This National Park Service website offers information and guides related to Reconstruction and the developing monuments and memorial sites, specifically in Beaufort County, South Carolina.

Videos

Reconstruction and 1876: Crash Course US History #22
https://www.youtube.com/watch?v=nowsS7pMApI&t

This video provides a brief overview of the Reconstruction Era.

US History # 10: The Reconstruction Era
https://www.youtube.com/watch?v=JKjE9CU06po

This Library of Alexandria video provides a presentation that reviews Reconstruction Era history.

Organizations

Beaufort History Museum at The Arsenal
713 Craven Street
Beaufort, SC 29902
(843) 379-3079
Website: https://beauforthistorymuseum.wildapricot.org/about

Originally built in 1789 to house artillery for the American Revolutionary War, The Arsenal on Craven Street now serves as a museum that explores 450 years of Beaufort's history. During Reconstruction, it served as the first Beaufort County voting station and as a storage facility for the Freedmen's Bureau.

Historic Mitchelville Freedom Park
229 Beach City Rd
Hilton Head Island, SC 29926
(843) 255-7301
Website: http://exploremitchelville.org

This organization provides visitors to the Freedom Park with the chance to explore one of the first established towns completely operated by freedmen, dating to 1862.

National Museum of African American History and Culture
1400 Constitution Ave NW
Washington, DC 20560
(844) 750-3012
Website: https://nmaahc.si.edu

This museum, part of the Smithsonian Institution, focuses on African American life in the United States from the first enslaved Africans brought here in the 1600s to the present day.

The National Museum of American History
1300 Constitution Ave NW
Washington, DC 20560
(202) 633-1000
Website: http://americanhistory.si.edu

This branch of the Smithsonian Institution covers the entirety of American history, including the Reconstruction Era.

The Penn Center
P.O. Box 126
16 Penn Center Circle West
St. Helena Island, SC 29920
(843) 838-2432
Website: http://www.penncenter.com

The Penn Center is an official part of the Reconstruction Era National Monument, which includes four locations around Beaufort County, South Carolina. Founded in 1862 as the Penn School, it was one of the first schools for formerly enslaved black people in the South.

Woodrow Wilson Family Home
1705 Hampton Street
Columbia, SC 29201
(803) 252-7742
Website: https://www.historiccolumbia.org/woodrow-wilson-family-home

This former home of President Woodrow Wilson features, according the organization's website, an interpretation of the "racial, social, and political landscape of Columbia and Richland County during the Reconstruction era."

INDEX

Page numbers in **boldface** refer to images.

ABOUT THE AUTHORS

Chet'la Sebree is a writer, editor, and researcher from the Mid-Atlantic. She has received degrees in English and writing from the University of Richmond and American University. She has worked on several books about US history, including the Courting History series for Cavendish Square Publishing. Her research focus is early American history.

Adriane Ruggiero has written numerous books about history, both ancient and modern, and international affairs, including books about the Ottoman Empire, the Great Depression, and both World Wars. She is also a frequent contributor to reference works such as *The Dictionary of the Middle Ages, The Encyclopedia of Ancient Greece and Rome*, and *Magill's Encyclopedia of Military History.*